# A Postcard from Rome

## DAVID HELWIG

VIKING

Published by the Penguin Group
Penguin Books Canada Ltd, 2801 John Street, Markham, Ontario, Canada L3R 1B4
Penguin Books Ltd, 27 Wrights Lane, London W8 5TZ
Viking Penguin Inc., 40 West 23rd Street, New York, New York 10010, U.S.A.
Penguin Books Australia Ltd, Ringwood, Victoria, Australia
Penguin Books (N.Z.) Ltd, 182-190 Wairau Road, Auckland 10, New Zealand
Penguin Books Ltd, Registered Offices: Harmondsworth, Middlesex, England

First published by Penguin Books Canada Limited, 1988

Printed in Canada

Canadian Cataloguing in Publication Data

Helwig, David, 1938–
        A postcard from Rome
    ISBN 0-670-82137-3

    I. Title.

    PS8515.E48P68  1988  C813'.54  C87-094824-5
    PR9199.3.H43P68  1988

59, 295

British Library Cataloguing in Publication Data Available
American Library of Congress Cataloguing in Publication Data Available

Research for this book was assisted by a short-term grant from the Canada Council.

# A Postcard from Rome

# Chapter 1

B flat chord, on cello, bass, trombone, bassoon. *Fortississimo, tutta forza.* Open fifth. Lacking the third, the tonality is ambiguous.

B flat triad, full orchestra.

A flat major.

Chord on E. Tonality ambiguous.

E major. Full chord, *tremolando*.

After the three bars of tremendous introductory chords, the curtain opens. The setting, the Jesuit church of Sant' Andrea della Valle, is high and golden, intricate with the excessive energies of the baroque – serving God with riches and complex artifice, with size and spectacle; it waits in ponderous bright grandeur for the first character to enter. This is the opening night of this production of *Tosca*, and the men and women in the *poltrone* are dressed in dinner-jackets and long dresses. Their faces are smooth and satisfied, set off by jewels and fabrics, revealed in a glow of light from the stage that is caught and reflected by the gold and red of the seats and boxes.

High in the theatre, a member of the claque, his seat in

the *galleria* provided by the tenor who is singing Cavaradossi, can't keep himself from muttering comments on
the unfolding performance to the American tourists who
sit beside him, though he has recently been threatened
with banishment from the theatre for this sort of thing.

"*Che fai?*"

*Il signor tenore* enters as Cavaradossi, the painter and
political idealist, in good voice, but not in the best of tem-
pers. The blue of his painter's smock is not what he had
hoped, too pale, and no one had warned him of the unflat-
tering effect at the dress rehearsal. It was only tonight in
the dressing-room that he became aware that this pale
blue made him look sallow. When he tried to adjust his
make-up to overcome the effect, he looked like a clown.
Now he stands with his back to the audience, pretending
to stare at Cavaradossi's picture of the soppy blue-eyed
Magdalen. How can one give any dignity to a character
who would paint that? Always, at this moment, he worries
that the prop miniature of Tosca will not be in the pocket
of his smock when he reaches for it. Once, an antagonized
properties mistress placed in his pocket a miniature on
which she had written a pointed and obscene insult.
He took it out, just as he was about to begin "*Recondita
armonia*," turning to the audience as he looked at it and
comprehended its message. And had come close to missing his entry.

In a small staff washroom inside a door just along a narrow corridor from the *guardaroba*, one of the ushers puts
a bottle of white wine in a sink and turns on the cold tap,
hoping to get the wine decently cool in the next half hour.
His girl works in a clothing store a few blocks along the Via
Tasso, and she has arranged to come and meet him here.

"*Ah! il mio sol pensier sei tui! Tosca, sei tu!*"

The American couple are startled at the enthusiasm of the applause for this expression of Cavaradossi's passionate love from the thin man beside them. Feeling it must be right, they join in.

The sacristan departs, leaving Cavaradossi alone to work on his Magdalen. Carefully the escaped political prisoner, Angelotti, comes out of the Attavanti chapel and reveals himself to the painter. Then, suddenly, Tosca's voice is heard from offstage, outside the locked doors of the church.

"Mario! Mario! Mario!"

The falling fourths are blurred, slightly toneless, almost a form of *Sprachgesang*, and the more critical members of the audience are a little startled. Is this to be some revolutionary version of the heroine?

Once Angelotti has hidden himself again, the door opens, and the soprano enters, her gown a deep rust colour, a bouquet of white and golden flowers in her arms, the bouquet that the naïve and heroic Tosca brings to present to the Virgin. She is not a young Tosca by any means, but she is well kept, moves with athletic energy, almost too quickly, as if she were pursued, and while she looks suspiciously around the stage she is avoiding the eyes of the tenor, but repeatedly seeking those of the conductor.

Cavaradossi is startled at the vigour with which his partner thrusts him away when he tries to embrace her. It is unlike anything that has occurred in rehearsals. She moves insistently to the front of the stage, and he follows her, convinced that she is trying to take the stage from him, destroy him. If it's to be war, he'll give a good account of himself.

By the end of the four bars of triplets, the conductor knows what he is seeing in the soprano's eyes, which seek his and hold them. It is panic he is seeing. He has observed it once or twice before, mostly in very young singers. If he can nurse her through a few bars, singing her entries quietly along with her, conducting from memory and never losing her eyes, she will probably come out of it. He ignores the tenor, who will survive on his own.

She begins her opening passages of recitative, both the pitch and the tone precarious, a frantic energy propelling her as she tries, by an act of will, to hold the stage, to survive.

The conductor sings louder in his raspy baritone, hoping to calm her, make her feel that he will get her through it somehow. He knows that the audience can hear him, but that no longer seems to matter. Remembers the story of the first Vienna performance of *Die Meistersinger*, when the tenor singing Hans Sachs, terrified by the hostility in the audience, lost his voice, leaving the conductor to sing as well as beat time. That was bad enough; but a baritone Tosca? The tenor is looking startled and confused and beginning to push his voice; when in doubt, sing louder.

On her first high A, the voice is close to breaking. Once more she begins a kind of speaking-the-notes-at-pitch. There are one or two hisses from the audience as she goes and kneels in front of the Madonna, her face in her hands, her body clenched like a fist.

Three bars. Time for her to get up, turn to Cavaradossi. She does not move. The conductor slows the tempo for the rest of the passage that leads to her next recitative,

which is begun without accompaniment. The passage
ends. He stares at the orchestra and has them hold the
final eighth for an eternity. The tenor moves toward her.
At last she stands, turns to the audience, appears to say
something and runs from the stage. The tenor stands in
blank silence. The audience begins to move and whisper.
The conductor watches it all, helpless.

# Chapter 2

*Dear Edith,*

    *There's no easy way to do this. I know because I've tried. A hundred times or so. Lost my courage every time.* Non posso, *I'd say to myself, and quit. I wasn't desperate enough yet. This time I'll do it. I'll send you this letter. I don't want to die without getting in touch.*

    *You must have thought I was dead years ago. I nearly died. I'd like to tell you about it some day.*

    *Maybe I'll get up the nerve to come and see you, but I'm not sure if you'll want to see me.*

    *This may be a shock, maybe you won't even believe it's true, but it is. I'm your father, Ralph, and I'm alive, here in Italy. All these years. I've seen stories in the* giornali *about you. Even pictures. Until I saw the pictures I thought the singer I read about might be some other Edith Fulton, but once I saw the pictures I knew.*

    *I don't want to die without getting in touch.*

    *I don't know what else there is to say.*

*Ralph Fulton*

# Chapter 3

Already now, for an hour or more, she had heard the sound of trams. The noises of night − doors opening, closing, the high-heeled shoes of a whore arriving and then leaving − had become the sound of morning, the trams, a bird singing.

Even here in the middle of the city. Singing.

There was a little light coming in the louvred shutters, a grey sad light. A long high room with rounded corners. Like a tea-caddy, a tin tea-caddy that her mother had used − no, not her mother, but Vi who lived next door. A long high room. Like a biscuit tin. Or a tomb.

Edith was within, the lid closed.

The trams were more frequent now.

She felt her heart beating. Somewhere in her brain was a small, persistent, invisible creature who wished her heart to beat and said now, now, now as it had for more than fifty years.

Now. Rest. Now. Rest. Now. Rest. Would you notate it as two-four or four-four?

Long glass curtains grey with age or dirt. Yellow walls, a sink, a bidet.

Dust. She pulled the covers over her head. There was no reason to get up. She did not exist. There was no reason to get up.

Footsteps in the hall. Doors. A woman's voice, flat, deep, repeating a single word, in an ugly contralto chant.

"*Asciugamani. Asciugamani. Asciugamani.*"

No one came with the towels, and the voice began again.

Edith lay in bed, empty, helpless. Something unthinkable had overtaken her during that performance of *Tosca,* and she had run off the stage, left the theatre, caught a train for Milan. To hide. Here in the city where she had come to study so long ago, in the rainy autumn, young, lost.

"*Asciugamani. "Asciugamani.*

Like a foghorn, But this time it brought footsteps from the porter's apartment.

She listened to them pass, as if there were some terrible high significance in the sound, then turned on her other side and pretended to sleep. There was a burning in her sinuses, and she found herself breathing, swallowing, testing the discomfort, but it was only habit now. It didn't matter. She was no longer the slave of tongue and palate and sinuses and the Greek twins, larynx and pharynx, and last night, after listening to Elizabeth's recital, hidden in the unnumbered seats of the top gallery, unable to see the stage, unable to be seen, she had come down the long sets of stairs, one after another, to the rainy street, and walked over to the bar on the corner and ordered red wine, one glass and then another.

She had thought it would feel daring to abuse the instrument, to drink the red wine as a symbol of her new freedom, but she could not stop watching the men and women who came into the bar from the theatre, afraid that one of them might recognize her and cry out "Signora Fulton." Full Tone. Fool Tone. No one recognized her. She stood in this bar less than a hundred feet from La Scala where she had many years before made her debut singing that pious prig Michaela, and the men and women dressed in Milanese good taste, who had listened to the recital by her friend and rival, Elizabeth, clustered together and sought the bartender's attention and ignored her.

The red wine, with its load of histamines, had done its work, and her sinuses were burning, the vocal cords thick.

It didn't matter. Her body was the average body of a woman in middle age. For thirty years, she had trained it to its freakish function, made it the servant of that disease of the throat, her voice, her only home the mountainous landscape between the opening bars and closing bars of a piece of music.

And now?

Free from the tyranny of the instrument, she was homeless, had come back to Milan because this was where she landed when she came to Italy, where she had put herself into the hands of *il maestro*, Tanzini, those rough, strong capable hands, that shaped and stroked and prodded. She was just so much singing meat, so much clay to be shaped into a performer.

There were three of them in those days, women of almost the same age, studying with Tanzini; Elizabeth, with her strapping build and always slightly hazy voice, little Giudetta who was somehow too gentle for it all, and Edith, whatever it was she had been. Tanzini called them *Le Mie Tre Grazie*, his Three Graces.

Giudetta had married and given up singing. Elizabeth, whose voice, it seemed to Edith, had never come entirely clear, was singing a recital at La Scala.

And Edith?

She had run from her ghosts, run bravely and run fast, but now they had caught her. So she had come back to Milan, to the neighbourhood of cheap hotels and *pensioni* where she had first lived. She had returned to Milan as if she might start over, as if she might find something here that would tell her where to go next.

Signora Full Tone. Signora Fool Tone.

There were people here she could visit, but she would avoid them all, unable to bear their sympathy, their polite inquiries about the nightmare in the Teatro Donizetti at Bergamo, or their polite refusal to make inquiries, the evasiveness of the sane confronting the mad.

Signora Fool Tone.

She could talk to no one, not even Ezio. He would be looking for her. The moment he heard, he would have begun trying to phone, sending telegrams, summoning her to Rome, offering to come and fetch her, but the naked unbearable humiliation was too much. Like Saint Some-body, she had been flayed, and without skin she did not care to be seen.

Outside, the noises of the city were making the state-ment of full day. Across the road, the matronly prosti-tutes would have taken up their positions under a small arcade. They were Edith's age, respectably dressed. She might have been one of them. There were many speciali-zations of the body, the soccer player, the whore, the singer, any of them could be left with nothing to take the place of what the body had lost.

It isn't really over, Ezio would say to her if he found her; she could hear the sound of his voice, intelligent, reassuring, surprisingly deep for such a tiny man. She could see the careful beard, the bright eyes. If she told him about the letter, about the startling, incomprehensible news that her dead father was apparently alive, he would say that of course that was the reason, and he would set out to find someone to take a chance and hire her again.

But it was over. *La commedia è finita.* Thirteen, fatherless, stricken with some shapeless insatiable desire, she had crouched by the radio on Saturday afternoons to listen to the opera broadcasts and weep. Poor Canio, poor Nedda, poor Tosca, poor Violetta, poor Edith. But it had all ended when she had walked on stage into that deaf echoing horror at Bergamo.

And now?

Nothing. The earth had opened, and she had fallen into the chasm that appeared; perhaps she was still falling – a little figure in long shot, an articulated dummy deceiving the camera, intercut with the terrified face of the screaming heroine, shot in close-up against a moving background. The heroine fell or was captured by the enemy or locked in the haunted house and waited, poor passive thing, for rescue. She had, after all the years of forcing life to her will, become a heroine of romance, paralysed, waiting for assistance. Her life had broken up into shots not yet cut together, a series of long shots, a woman arriving in Milan by train, unattached to the world, noticing only odd facts – that the signal bell on the Metro used the falling interval of an augmented fourth – a woman walking into a cheap *pensione*, unrelated close-ups, a woman in the far corner of the top gallery of La Scala, listening, a look of strain on her face, a woman lying in bed, her ageing face puffy from sleep, her eyes blank and yet horrified.

A woman alone on stage, her body held straight, her mouth wide, as if singing.

It was over, and she was not ready. Ezio, dear soul, had been trying to get her to prepare, had talked her into taking those small acting parts in movies, a rude woman in a restaurant, a pious mother, a murder suspect, with the idea, obviously, that he was helping her toward a new career. He had taken her into editing rooms – his money was invested and he could get permission – and she had been horrified at the pieces of film that hung there like moments of life disassembled, taken to pieces as a child might demolish a toy.

How was one to prepare? Marry, buy a house some-where? Those things had not been part of her life. She could not understand them. She had always been alone; the first crucial decisions had somehow been out of her control, and from then on she had simply worked out her fate. She lived in hotel rooms and borrowed apartments; there were human beings on the fringes, Ezio in Rome, in London Milton and Mildred who were her agents, a few singers worth having dinner with, conductors and theatre managers who handled her, with the professional *savoir-faire* that made them seem like undertaker's men at a not very sad funeral.

Her closest companion was her voice; it was a brilliant, cosseted, tender, almost sickly child, in need of constant attention, but now and then rewarding its loving servant with sudden cleverness, a precocious and charming insight. And at times it was her friend, reliable, interesting. And it was her lover; it made her body shine and vibrate and swell with blood and oxygen; it hummed in her spine and skull like a long slow unending orgasm.

But something in her had served this child, this friend, this lover, with papers demanding a separation, the red wine a token, like staying out all night without explanation. Communication had broken down, as they liked to say in the pages of vulgar advice to the unhappily married. There were so many at it these days; she had once blundered on an ad in the yellow pages of some strange American city: Family Therapy and Divorce Medication.

The pieces of film hung on little wire hooks. A child in a field of grass. An adolecent girl, proudly silent. A young woman laughing. A woman alone on stage, her mouth open wide, as if singing.

She needed Divorce Medication for this severing from her child, her lover; there was no longer the trust in her that she could give what was required, that she could surrender herself. Something in her froze at the sight of the child; something in her went stiff at the lover's touch. Panic, and no deliberate control, no act of will could help.

She held her breath and listened to the sounds in the hall, the sounds in the street; she could hear perfectly, yet on that stage, she could suddenly perceive only a meaningless disorder of noise, and she could never return to a stage without knowing that it might happen again.

Two more years, that had been her plan, perhaps three or four if the voice held up and she was able to find some new roles. The Contessa in *Figaro*, perhaps Donna Elvira, and most of all, perhaps the Marschallin. She had set Milton and Mildred to looking for an engagement to do *Rosenkavalier*. If she kept herself in good condition, it would be a role to sing and retire on.

She had made her plan, to prepare for an amicable separation. But instead, it was done, all at a blow. It had been taken out of her hands.

And now? Wait in silence for this man who claimed to be her lost father? Sing for coins outside the cafés of Piazza Navona?

Crouched in a chair in that dressing-room in Bergamo, she had sworn that she would never sing again, never open her mouth to let a note emerge. Inevitable at that moment, but what was to fill the space where singing had been?

She could dress and go out to join the prostitutes across the road, bring her clients here, tip the porter, and return to this bed while the man did his business on her. She was in a fit state for humiliation, though the women looked bored, business-like, confident, not a bit humiliated; perhaps the clients were at their mercy. Who knew? Who had the power, the singer or the audience?

To be singing *Tosca* when it happened; a character she had always loved. Tosca, the diva, the woman of feeling and power created by Sardou for the magical Bernhardt. Tosca was so much alone, that was why Edith had loved her. Yes, she had her beautiful boy artist, but one knew that however much she would sacrifice for him, underneath it all she was solitary. She was all capital letters, Love and Art and Death; those were the companions of her solitude.

Edith lay on her back and stared up into the tea-caddy, the biscuit tin, that contained her. How long could she stay here? Her mother had always suspected that she would come to a bad end. Was this it? Perhaps she would hide away until she had no money left and then become a beggar in a church porch, hand out, mumbling.

Sooner or later, she supposed, she must return to the apartment in old Rome, but once she did, she must face a human being, for Ezio would be watching from his window across the *viale*.

But she could not return there. She was flayed like Saint Somebody. She had no skin.

# Chapter 4

Ezio had been waiting for her, as she knew he would – a note pinned to her door and, scarcely ten minutes after her arrival, a knock. Ezio had lived in this neighbourhood for years, and he had pressed into service as spies all his acquaintances, the hardware merchants and booksellers, the waiters at every *trattoria,* the stall-holders at the market.

So he had arrived at her door, his narrow aristocratic face poised and calm, and she had refused to talk to him. He knew, already, that she had phoned London and told Milton and Mildred to cancel all her bookings, and, when Mildred had attempted to remonstrate, hung up the phone. Now, when Ezio attempted to talk sense to her, she sulked, and after a few minutes he began to speak to her in English instead of Italian – the only sign he ever gave of being angry with her.

For a week after she had come back she refused to tell him anything. They had lunch together, and he went on speaking to her in English, as if she were some kind of tourist.

*"Parla italiano,"* she said to him finally.

"I shall speak Italian," he said, "when we have something to say."

Half irritated, half amused, she began to talk about what had happened at Bergamo, the panic, the strange sudden inability to hear her own voice accurately or to discriminate clearly the sounds of the music around her. After lunch they went back to his apartment, and he sat down at the piano and demanded that she sing.

She refused, then tried to explain to him that even if she could sing quite normally here it would make no difference. After that failure, that terrible humiliation on stage, she no longer had the resources to perform in public. Something in her had broken as she stood on that stage, as lost and helpless as an amateur. There was no escape from the knowledge that it might happen again.

He let her go, and for the next few days she went through the motions of her life, but it was all lived in a punishing underworld of arbitrary and meaningless action now that the centre of her life, the work that gave it meaning, was gone. She woke late in the mornings, spent hours gazing out over the roof-tops of the neighbourhood, cooked elaborately, then could not eat the food. At the bottom of a drawer, under a pile of other correspondence, was the letter that made her watch every old man in the street, half expecting one of them to seize her and claim to be the man who had written it. Her father. No, her father was dead. One of the lost. Her lost father and her lost son. And now her life, her career, her beloved voice. All gone.

On the wall of her kitchen was taped a postcard-sized print of a painting by Kees van Dongen. She had seen the original years ago in New York just after a couple of mediocre concerts in New England and a disastrous audition for Rudolf Bing at the Metropolitan. Bing had been uninterested from the first moment, and as a result she had sung badly, and the next day, finding the painting in a gallery, she had been bitterly amused by its garish colours and cruel portraiture. *Modjesko, Soprano Singer.* Chromeyellow skin, the head in profile with fat scarlet lips agape. On the head, some bizarre conglomeration of pink and green and blue that was coiffure and chapeau. The left hand clasping the left breast.

She had bought the postcard in a mood of bitterness, but over the years, as it followed her from place to place, she had grown almost fond if it; now once again it mocked her. The singer as fat fool.

The buzzer brought her quickly down the stairs to the apartment door, which opened on a small, often disorderly courtyard. The furniture-repair man stored odds and ends of wood and metal and one of the other tenants a motorbike. It was a cool grey day, and two young people stood there, against a background of rubbish and wooden doors and old plaster walls, looking misplaced, unsuitable, spruce and uneasy, the young woman's face shaped by the recipe for a smile, the young man nervously intent, his bright brown eyes restless.

They were obviously strangers, North American, and yet she felt something about them not quite right, the girl's plaid kilt and white nylon blouse, the man's tweed jacket and brown trousers, cut a bit too short. An air of unembarrassed brightness. What world had they come from?

"Yes?" Edith said. "Can I do something for you?" She wondered momentarily – their arrival was so odd – if speaking English might be a mistake.

"I have an appointment," the girl said, "to sing for you."

"Do you?"

"I phoned," the girl said, "from Toronto. My teacher told me to. And Faith Riordan."

"You phoned me?"

"Last month. You said I could come and sing for you. That you might help me find a teacher. Or teach me yourself."

Edith searched, finally remembered. It was the kind of thing she would usually have turned down, but Faith's name could always turn the key. Faith was ancient now, imprisoned in a wheelchair, her handwriting shaky and distorted, but she still had a sharp mind, a sharp ear, and Edith owed her so much that anyone sent by Faith must be admitted. But now? When she was all in pieces?

"I don't teach," she said, and wondered why she was still convinced of that. She couldn't sing. What else was there for her? What else?

"I don't teach," she repeated, inanely. She had, perhaps, lost her mind.

The two figures that faced her were almost the same height. There was something bent about the man's shoulders, something guarded in the posture of his whole body, a small brown animal, afraid, yet when his eyes flickered toward Edith they were shining, as if with the discovery that she might be good to eat. The woman's face was open, even a shade empty, good enough features, with a superficial animation.

"You said you'd listen. I phoned to ask." Baldly insistent.

"Are you staying in Rome?" Edith asked, unable to think of anything else. She wanted Ezio to sense what was happening from his apartment across the little street and

to come here and send them away so that Edith could be
alone to lie with a pillow over her head and grieve over her
barren life.

"Yes. We're here for a year. I told you about it on the
telephone."

The girl kept bringing up the telephone as if the instrument had magic powers. Edith didn't like the telephone.
She tried to recall the story she must have been told, but
couldn't. She had been on the way out the door, hurrying
to catch a train to Bergamo to begin rehearsing *Tosca*, and
she had only half listened. Presumably she had written
this appointment in her book, but now that appointment
book was meaningless, and she had lost it.

"Can I sing for you?"

No. No. No. You can't sing for me. I don't want to hear
another singer's voice. I don't want to know that you are
young and full of self-confidence. I'm a dead woman. Let
me be.

Edith stared at the pair of them and was about to make
an excuse, something fatuous, something brutally dis-
honest, but she studied their clothes, the smile that never
left the girl's face, and she relented.

"Come upstairs, then."

Inside she directed them to the piano. Get it done.
There were a dozen reputable teachers in Rome, even
some good ones who spoke English. Listen to the girl and
send her away.

"I'm Nancy," the girl said abruptly, as she took music
from an old-fashioned briefcase, "and this is my husband, Lee."

Lee was sitting on the piano bench, the music spread
out in front of him.

"I thought I'd sing —"
Edith interrupted.
"Don't tell me," she said. "Just sing."
She hated the girl. She hated the pair of them. She felt
they had been sent to persecute her. She hated this Nancy's
broad hips and upright posture, the deadly accurate way
Lee's fingers fell on the piano keys. Awkward refugees
from nowhere, come to intrude on her privacy.

*Ach, ich fühl's, es ist verschwunden,*
*Ewig hin die liebe Glück.*

She might have known. Damn Faith. Damn her. It was
(damn her!) an extraordinary voice, pure and accurate and
with a wonderful floating quality. It seemed to hang in
the air, without effort, to sustain beyond the possibility of
a voice to sustain. All the more she hated this young
woman and her brown-rabbity husband with his quick
eyes. Edith was afraid, almost, that the beauty of Mozart's
music, along with her own anger and sense of imprison-
ment, the desire to leap from the chair and run, and the
way the bright voice caressed the notes, would make her
cry. She looked out a window and saw a corner of a roof-
top garden. Think of something. Name the plants.
Nameless.
She could only command herself to sit still as the voice
wound serenely about the music. It was almost emotion-
less. Eerie, that beauty without effort or commitment. It
was a rare voice, and the girl sang almost as if she had no
idea of its quality.

*Fühlst du nicht der Liebe Sehnen,*
*So wird Ruh im Tode sein.*

The last phrase hung in the air, and the man at the piano began to shift sheets of music. Edith stood up. She couldn't bear any more.

"It's a very beautiful voice," she said. "It's an exceptional voice."

The husband was staring at her from the piano, his eyes careful.

"It's a gift of God," he said. "God has touched Nancy and placed his gift in her body."

It was the first time he had spoken.

"Are you a Christian?" he said.

"No," Edith said. She did not tell him that in her lost, empty state she sometimes dropped into the old churches as she wandered through Rome, and if she saw a priest waiting in the confessional always felt a ridiculous impulse – something as immediate and inexplicable as the impulse to jump over a cliff when one stood close – to enter the confessional and start to babble. She knew it wasn't a religious impulse, only a vertiginous desire to blab, to talk about herself, to tell her story. She wondered whether, if she did, the priest would tell her to stop trying to make herself interesting, that she was only seeking an audience.

"Nancy and I are committed Christians," the man was saying.

"Just what does that mean? In practice? To a singer?"

"We recognize the hand of God in every circumstance of our lives. We listen for the voice of God and ask him to guide us every step of our way. We aren't ashamed to confess Christ. Every day of our lives we're aware of being touched by the endless outpouring of his grace."

"And the voice of God has brought you to my apartment, has it?"

"In a sense, yes. I came to Rome to seek Christ through

his apostles who travelled to Rome and died here. I came
to learn about the early Christian community. To go down
into the darkness of the catacombs and see the sparks
that were struck there."

"A vivid metaphor."

"I have dozens of vivid metaphors. They're signs of God's
grace. New ones come to me every day. Just this morning
I saw how Christianity was a benign parasite that grew
within the putrefying body of old Rome and brought the
body back to new life."

"Vivid, certainly."

"Vivid means full of life. To be full of God is to be full of
life."

"And you're here to study."

"I'm here to see the academic study of archaeology put
to present use. To make the stones speak to men."

"And as for you?" Edith said to the girl.

"Since Lee was coming to Rome," she said, "I thought it
would be a chance to improve my singing. There are so
many great Italian opera singers."

It was empty and proper and pious. Edith wanted to slap
the pasty face and bring some colour into it. Would this
commonplace girl have anything in her large enough for
opera? Could she make herself into one of the divine and
tragic whores? Opera was a bordello. There was no place
in it for this smiling girl who knuckled under to her husband's soft tyranny. Edith remembered how his fingers
pressed mechanically on the piano keys and imagined
them pressing, with the same touch, the girl's flesh. It
made her shudder.

"Shall I sing something else?" the girl said.

"No. That was enough. It's a good voice."

The husband was packing away the music. The girl was
staring toward Edith, and for a moment there was some
expression on her face, something behind the cheerful
smile. She looked almost frightened.

"I want to study with you," she said.

"Why?"

"I just know I do."

"The voice of God, is it?"

The girl looked away, confused, and for the first time
was altogether human. Suddenly Edith liked her, wanted
to put an arm around her, but not in the presence of her
Christian consort.

"Do you have a telephone number?" Edith said.

The man took out a small notebook and began to write.
He passed the paper to her.

"I'll have to think about this," Edith said.

It was early Saturday evening, and every bell in Rome was
tolling, the air of her apartment vibrating with the clamour.
Edith sat in her chair and looked at the book in her hand,
not reading. She remembered her teacher, Tanzini, who
always insisted that a singer should avoid books, that the
stimulation was too intellectual. He was firmly convinced
that books could damage the voice, and for years Edith
had felt a certain guilt at spending her free hours over
pages of print.

But now she was no longer a singer, she could read as
much as she pleased.

The noise of the bells ended. From the street below, she
heard voices, laughter.

Should she agree to teach Nancy Longridge? What else
was there? Sometimes Edith wondered about returning

to Canada, to the places where the story that was now ended had begun. In the meantime, she walked through strange sections of Rome. Sad, rainy gardens. Headless figures in the rain, bits of Roman buildings, funerary sculpture, a dingy Venus with a big behind, the gardens green and overgrown in the rainy light, the place for an elegiac love story. A few lonely carp, brown and orange, in a pond. Funerary stele of family groups. Blind staring eyes.

The previous afternoon, she and Ezio had walked by the Tiber, putting up with the traffic noise for the calming sight of the river.

"Have you started to sing?" he said.

"No."

"When will you start?"

"I've told you. I don't intend to sing again."

The wide river was the colour and texture of green olives. The city was beautiful and familiar, and yet she was homeless in it.

"You must sing," he said. "It is your life."

"Perhaps I can make a new life."

"It takes a long time to make a life."

She didn't answer.

"Especially for a singer."

She knew he was right. The body of a singer was perfected to its one function, sacrificed to certain startling abilities. Years of training, years of abnegation to be able to contain in the body the most extreme, most grandiose, most painful moments of human expressiveness.

"I hate to see you abandon what you have spent years learning."

"You've invested a lot of time and energy in me, Ezio, but now you'll have to find another singer to worry over.

I'm finished." It was a bitter remark, and he did not deserve it. But it had been said and could not be unsaid.

"There are many singers," he said.

"Yes."

He walked for a moment beside her without speaking. The traffic beside them on the Lungotevere was fast and loud.

"There are not so many friends," he said.

Edith reached out and took his arm.

# Chapter 5

Edith could hear a bobolink, its long, bubbling, gurgling song rolling through the air above her. From farther off came a thin whistle from some other bird. Edith lay with her face turned down into the grass where she could see nothing but the twilight world that took place down here, invisible except from close up. As she lay there, flat on her stomach, staring into the half darkness where the stems met the earth, the weeds and grass itched her bare legs, but she did not move. If someone saw her, a little girl lying on the ground, her face hidden, they would know that something tragic had happened.

From the other side of the fence she could hear the Dunfields' two Holsteins tearing and chewing grass; one had looked toward Edith as she walked past, then looked away and returned to cropping the grass, the heavy bag that hung beneath it filling with milk that Gerry Dunfield would strip off into a pail, the long teats nestled in his broad fingers. Edith liked the sweet smell of the cows and the fresh milk, but she didn't like Gerry Dunfield's jokes about how much milk she'd have when she grew up.

Tonight, after supper, she could walk down the road and watch Gerry Dunfield milk the two Holsteins. As if nothing had happened at all. No. She wouldn't go. She'd stay in her room.

Her mother had wept noisily all last night, and when Edith left the house she was crying again. Edith hadn't cried except when her father walked her down to the park and gave her the little silver heart pendant and told her to be good to her mother. They were sitting there together on a bench by the edge of the baseball diamond, her father in his army uniform, and she started to cry and cuddled against him, and she felt the rough fabric of the uniform scratch her cheek. Her father was talking about the war, Germany and England and Russia, and although she didn't follow it all she loved the sound of his voice when he was serious like this, and talked to her as if she were adult. Edith stared across the ball diamond, remembering how she and her mother had come to watch her father play second base, and the shouting when he'd hit the ball. He was saying that Verna didn't really understand the war, how he had to enlist.

"She's all right, Verna is, but there are things she just can't seem to get into her head. I can't make her see."

Edith was holding the little silver heart in her fist, afraid that she would drop it in the dust and it would be gone, and that if that happened her father would die. Hitler would kill him. If she kept the silver heart safe, her father would be safe too. She had put it away, wrapped in tissue, in a little box and put the box in the drawer with her socks and underpants, but she had to keep checking to see that it was still there. This afternoon, when her father walked away from the house, carrying his kitbag and not looking back, she watched him from the front porch until he turned the corner, and then she started to run to the corner, but instead she stopped, in front of Vi and Mabel's house, and stood still for a minute and then ran back to her own house and up to her room to check on the little silver heart, still safe, then looked out the window where her father had disappeared.

He was gone, the empty street speaking his absence, and Edith had raced down the road toward the Dunfields', and come into this field at the edge of the trees and thrown herself down, her head buried, away from the light. She imagined how she must look, a thin tragic figure, but no one came to observe her. The summer sun burned down on her back and legs, and she watched the insect world, which, close to her eyes, was huge and malign. The ants, the beetles, were metallic, insistent. She saw an ant carrying the dead body of another insect, and she started to think about the dead body, about death, the undertaker's big black car coming to get Vi and Mabel's mother, as Edith watched from her window and heard the terrible sound that Vi was making.

She felt sick, she wanted to be able to walk down Field Street and meet her father after he got off work at Bowman's Hardware, and the realization that she couldn't made her cry, cold frightened tears, not like the kind at the park when he gave her the present and talked about the war, those warm, almost comforting tears, held against his uniform. These tears were hard and icy and painful.

Edith got up to go home. The bobolink had stopped his song but, farther off, there were other birds calling across the warm afternoon. The Dunfields' Holsteins ate placidly, paying no attention to her. No one could see her here except maybe God or Jesus, and she didn't know much about them. Sometimes her Grandma Sinclair took her to church, but she could never make much sense of God and Jesus. Like Hitler, they existed a long way off.

When she got back to the house, it was quiet; perhaps her mother had gone out. Maybe she was over talking to Vi. Edith went to the sideboard and got out one of the old one-sided records that her father had bought second-hand from someone who brought them to the store. He'd paid two dollars for them, and her mother was shocked and angry, had stamped out of the house to go visit Grandma Sinclair, and even when Edith went to bed she hadn't returned. But she was back in the morning to make Edith's breakfast, pouring out cornflakes into the bowl with yellow flowers and milk from the blue pitcher, Edith aware that she was still mad because her father was talking too much and calling her "Vern."

The record Edith took out was one of their favourites, Marcella Sembrich singing "Caro nome"– the walking-downstairs song, she and her father called it – that was how the melody sounded, the voice starting at the top and walking carefully down, then going to the top of a different staircase and walking down that. Edith's picture of Marcella Sembrich was of a very tall, slender woman with long dark hair that glimmered in the candle-light as she moved: slowly down one silver staircase after another, with a tread so perfectly assured, so slow and beautiful, that only music could express it.

Edith lifted the heavy wooden top of the record-player and slid the black disc over the spindle and down. Usually when she did this her father was in his chair across the room, watching her to make sure she did it all correctly. She turned and looked at the empty chair, feeling that she ought to cry, but no tears came; instead she only turned back to the machine and lifted the arm to the edge of the record. There was the grinding, rubbing sound as she set the needle down, and then came the rush of the music.

Marcella Sembrich was walking with infinite elegance down the long silver stairs.

"You shut that thing off. You shut that off right now."

Her mother's voice was screaming at her, cutting past the lovely outpouring of the music, and when Edith turned toward the voice her mother was close to her, her hair, which always lay against her head in such soft careful waves or was tied back under a kerchief when she was cleaning the house, now stuck out in patches, as if she had been trying to tear it out with her hands. Her eyes were sore and her skin wet and flushed. Edith thought of baby birds she had found, wet and staring, their feathers unkempt, ugly things, unsuited to the world.

*She's all right, Verna is, but there are things she just can't seem to get into her head.* Edith remembered her father's words, but as her mother stood, staring, shouting, it seemed as if she had got too many things into her head, as if something in there was exploding, trying to burst out in shocks of hair, in tears, in screams of rage.

Her mother came closer and Edith drew back, afraid that she was going to be struck, but her mother went past her and grabbed the record off the turntable, a scratching sound as she dragged the arm off it, then lifted the record and dashed it on the floor.

"His damn records, his damn army. I hate him. I hate him."

She was stamping her right foot on the fragments of the record, smashing them, her foot hitting the floor with a maddened repetition.

"His damn records. Damn, damn, damn, damn."

Then she turned away, as if she knew that Edith was watching her and was stung by the awareness. For a second, she turned away, her back bent, and then she ran back to the bedroom, the door slamming behind.

The house was quiet, and somewhere far inside her ears Edith could hear the bright voice of Marcella Sembrich coming down the silver stairs. She looked at the black fragments on the floor that had once contained that sound, but now they were nothing but parts of a jigsaw puzzle. Her father turned the corner and vanished. Now his record was smashed. When he came back, he would want to take out that record and hear "*Caro nome*," and he would ask Edith where it was, but she wouldn't say. She would leave it to her mother to explain.

Suddenly, Edith was frightened that her mother had found the little silver heart and destroyed it too, or thrown it away, and she ran to her room and opened the drawer where it was hidden and unwrapped the tissue. It was still safe, but she was afraid that if she left it in the drawer her mother would find it when she put away the clean laundry. For now she would  put it back, covered with her underpants, but she knew she must find a place where it would never be discovered. She held it tight in her hand as she had at the park when her father gave it to her, and she looked out the window to the corner of Field Street, as if, by watching hard enough, she could conjure up his figure, see him coming back around the corner and approaching the house.

The street was empty and still in the hot sunlight, but then Vi's fat old dog came round the front of the house, sniffed a couple of bushes, lifted his leg, while, farther along, Mrs Creamer appeared from her front door, wearing a white dress and a white hat with blue flowers, and carrying a bag for her shopping.

She was going downtown.

Edith began to wonder whether her father might still be somewhere in town, standing at the station waiting for his train to arrive and take him to the war, or at the bus depot by McCarthy's drugstore. Or did the army come to get them in trucks or tanks or some kind of mysterious military vehicle? If she knew where he was waiting Edith could set off through the streets to find him, to see him once more before he disappeared to fight the Germans.

She could tell him what Verna had done to the record of Marcella Sembrich.

Edith lay down with her ear against the bedroom floor to try to hear if her mother was making any noise in her bedroom downstairs, but she couldn't hear anything except the soft sound of her ear scrunching against the wooden boards. Vi had a big sea shell, rough and covered with sharp points on the outside, but soft and pink and smooth inside the lip, and if Vi held it to your ear, you could hear the distant sound of waves falling on the seashore. Vi said that was the sound of the shell remembering the ocean.

Down the block, in the shade of one of the elms that surrounded the Woodrow house, Edith could see Kenny Woodrow playing with cars. She could walk down and join him, but she didn't feel like playing with him right now, yet she didn't want to stay in the house, knowing that her mother was nearby, silent and angry, full of the mysterious grief that held her in its grip.

Edith decided to go and visit Vi. She went quietly down the stairs, afraid that her mother would come out of the bedroom to scream at her, but there was no sound, and Edith opened the front door and went into the heat of the afternoon, the sunlight baking the clay of the front lawn, the grass thin and yellow. Would her mother have to cut the grass now, and dig the garden, and do all her father's jobs? Sometimes Edith tried to push the lawn-mower, but it was too heavy for her; she needed her father's help.

Vi was dressed up when she opened the door, in a maroon dress with white swirls all through it, and patent-leather shoes with low heels. Her sister Mabel went out to work every day at Fullerton's Insurance, but Vi stayed home and looked after the house – wrapped in a loose flowered house dress, her hair in a white kerchief until she finished her work, and then she'd get dressed up and wait for Mabel to arrive home. She was a big woman, and the door was filled with her strong maroon presence.

"Well, here's Edith come to visit us."

She talked as if they were both there, even when Mabel was away at work. Vi stood back from the door and Edith walked into the hall. The blinds were drawn against the heat, and the house, which was always dark and crowded with heavy polished furniture and plates and dishes and souvenirs of the trips that Vi and Mabel's parents had taken – the sea shells and ruby-glass pitchers with the names on and strangely shaped ashtrays that no one used – was even more dim and close than usual. In the hallway, where Edith stood, was the tall black piano, the top covered with photographs in gold and silver frames.

"Did you come to play the piano?" Vi said.

"No," Edith said, "not today."

"Shall we get a cookie?"

"Yes, please."

"Made some icebox cookies this morning."

She led the way to the kitchen, took a cookie jar down from a shelf and set it on the red and white oilcloth on the table, then took out a plate and put some cookies on it.

"Shall we take them into the front room?"

Vi always said this and Edith always agreed. The front room was the room for company, where the sea shell was, and the plates from Niagara Falls. Edith sat on a straight chair close to the sea shell, and Vi settled into her big chair in the corner. Edith started to eat her cookie, and quickly it was gone and she reached out to the plate for another one. She knew Vi wouldn't mind.

"Hungry today," Vi said. "Didn't you eat lunch?"

With her father leaving and her mother crying, Edith hadn't thought about lunch.

"I forgot," she said.

"All the excitement."

"I guess."

"Verna will feel better after a good cry," Vi said. She knew that Edith's mother had been crying; she must have heard her. Sometimes her mother said that Vi peeked in their windows from up in her bedroom.

"Did you cry?" Vi said.

"Just a little."

"Do you want to come and sit on Vi's lap and have a good cry?"

Edith didn't know what to say, so she didn't answer.

"You come and sit on Vi's lap."

Edith got up and went to her, not sure that she wanted to, but unable to say no. Vi lifted her onto her lap and put her arms around her and began to rock her. Above her, she saw Vi's face close to her. She had a red nose and a moustache and there was a strange warm sweetish smell that came from her mouth. She was kissing Edith on the hair and rocking her.

"You just have a good cry," her voice was saying, and even though Edith didn't want to cry she found that tears were coming. The sound of Vi's words was making them come.

"Don't you worry if your Daddy's gone away. Vi will look after you. Vi will look after her sweet little girl."

Edith wanted to stop crying, but she just couldn't. She felt something wet on her arm and she saw that tears were coming out of Vi's shut eyes and falling from her face onto Edith and onto the arm of the chair. Edith was hot and frightened, imprisoned in Vi's strong arms here in this dim silent room. She saw a tear come down Vi's face and through her moustache onto her lip, and a tongue came out to lick it away. But still Edith couldn't stop her own tears from coming. She didn't know what she was crying about, just somehow she couldn't stop.

"Vi will look after her sweet little girl, her little Edith."

It was almost like music the way she was saying the words, rocking Edith back and forth. The mirror over the fireplace reflected the lamp of green glass that hung in the centre of the room and, as Vi moved, the lamp seemed to be swaying back and forth. The whole room was in motion, the sea shell with its shining pink surface, the shelf with the ruby-glass pitcher, the amber-glass pickle cruet and the china vase with pheasant feathers, all the cups on the polished surface of the sideboard that looked so much like a coffin on legs that Edith had been afraid, after Vi's mother died, that she might be still inside there, preserved like everything else in this house, clean and shined and ancient.

Vi stopped moving and crooning and sat up. She held Edith away from her, and her voice changed.

"Well," she said, "that's better, isn't it?"

Edith wasn't sure if it was better at all. Her face was still wet with her own tears and her arm with Vi's, but Vi lifted her efficiently off her lap and set her on the floor, took a hanky out of the sleeve of her dress and wiped Edith's face dry.

"Shall we have a look at the scrapbook?" she said.

Edith couldn't quite talk; the room was still swaying, and all the red and green and amber of the coloured glass was too intense, too liquid and vibrant.

"Or do you want to hear Harry Lauder?" Vi said.

"No," Edith said. "Not today."

She was afraid that Vi would play "Stop Your Ticklin', Jock," and tickle her until she was frantic, the way she did sometimes. She knew she couldn't stand that, not today; she thought she might start to cry again, to bawl like a baby at the mere thought of that tickling.

"Have another cookie," Vi said, "and I'll get the scrapbook."

Edith took a cookie in her hand, but she wasn't sure she could eat it, though she didn't dare put it back on the plate. Quickly she stuffed it in her mouth and munched with determination on the dryness of it. She got most of it down before Vi came back down the stairs.

"Come and sit on the love-seat," Vi said.

That was where they always sat to look at the scrapbook.

It was a love-seat, Edith always assumed, because Vi sat there to do things she loved to do, like listening to Lux Radio Theatre or looking at the scrapbook. Side by side, with the book, which had a Union Jack on the cover, spread across their knees, they studied the pages.

At the front were the pictures of Winston Churchill looking fierce and telling how he was going to beat Hitler. Then came the flowers, mostly roses, all neatly cut out and pasted in place, then the King and Queen and Princess Elizabeth and Princess Margaret Rose. Princess Margaret Rose was Vi's favourite, and there was one page with a picture of her alone, and all around the little girl Vi had pasted tiny pink roses that she found on wrapping for a baby shower.

After Princess Margaret Rose came the part of the scrapbook that Edith liked best, where Vi had collected the most interesting pictures from Ripley's Believe It or Not in the Toronto *Star*, wonderful phenomena like the legless dancer and the Hindu who had hung from a wire for thirty-eight years and the man who attached bells to his eyebrows and could play tunes. Sometimes, after Edith had looked at the book with Vi, she would go home and tell her father the things she had seen, and together they would discuss what local oddities they might record and send to Mr Ripley.

Tonight her father wouldn't be there to ask what she'd found in Vi's scrapbook. There would only be the silence from the bedroom and the pieces of the shattered record. When Edith remembered that, she felt cold and frightened again.

"I have to go, Vi," Edith said.

"But we're not finished the book. There's some new Believe It or Not."

"I have to go. I told my mother I'd come right back."

"Don't tell lies, Edith."

"I did. I told her I'd come back right away."

"I guess you don't like the scrapbook any more," Vi said.

"I do. I like it, but I have to go."

Edith had got up from the love-seat and was standing on the red and gold swirl of the carpet. The sun had just started to shine against a corner of the drawn blind, and Edith could see little specks of dust in the air. Vi was staring at her as if she was mad, but then she smiled. Her teeth were small, with spaces between.

"Well, I guess this is a pretty special day, your daddy going to join the army and all. But we had a good cry about it, didn't we? Don't you worry. Your daddy and all the other Canadian boys will go over there and give those Germans what for."

Edith was moving toward the door.

"Thank you for the cookies," she said.

When she went out Vi was still sitting on the love-seat, but, in case she went to the window to watch, Edith pretended to run home, round to the back door, but when she was out of sight of Vi's house she went through the empty lot and down the road toward the Dunfields' place until she came to Pigott Street, where she turned, planning to go round the block and arrive at the Woodrows' house where she hoped to find Kenny still playing in the yard. She didn't want to go home, and she didn't want to be at Vi's any more, and lying alone in the field had frightened her.

When she got to Kenny's house, he was still playing with

his cars in the dusty earth under the swing set. Edith stood by the picket fence and looked in at him. He had a smooth face, with pale eyes and hair and hardly any eyebrows, it made him look almost transparent, something that was both reassuring and uncomfortable to look at. Edith watched him over the fence and wondered how long she could stand here before he realized that she was watching him. Just then he looked up at her, as if he'd already known, had only been waiting for that thought to come into her mind. Edith didn't like it when she had ideas like that, it was too confusing.

"You coming in?" Kenny said.

Edith nodded and walked to the gate, then across the lawn to the place where Kenny was playing. When she got there, he started to explain to her what all the cars were, and the roads he had made. He'd been there all afternoon and he had it all worked out.

"You can have this one," he said giving her a small brown car, "it's an army car."

"My father joined the army."

"I know. My mother said. My father can't because he has to look after the store."

Edith began running her car down one of Kenny's roads. Her father was in the car, going to meet Winston Churchill, because he was such a good soldier that Winston Churchill wanted to make him a general. The car drove slowly because it was such an important occasion.

"You can't go on that road," Kenny said.

"Why not?"

"That's my road for the truck. The army cars can't go on it."

"It's going to see Winston Churchill."

"Who's he?"

"You don't even know?"

"Who is he?"

"He's the prime minister of England."

"So?"

"He's fighting against Hitler."

"Everybody's fighting against Hitler."

"But Winston Churchill is the boss."

"My father's the boss at the store. Then I'm going to be the boss."

"I'm going to be a singer like Marcella Sembrich."

Edith wasn't sure where that idea had come from, but once she'd said it, it seemed right, as if she might have been thinking it without knowing she was.

"Who's she?"

"She's a singer. She sings *Caro nome*." We have a record."

"What's she sound like?"

Edith took a breath and tried an imitation.

"That sounds stupid," Kenny said.

The words hurt. Edith had been pleased with how she sounded.

"You don't even know who Winston Churchill is," she said and went back to running the car along one of the roads through the dust. Not only Winston Churchill was waiting to meet her father, but King George as well. Maybe even the Queen.

"You want to watch me pee?" Kenny said.

Edith recognized this as an apology for being mean.

"OK."

Kenny got up, and she followed him around the side of the house past his mother's vegetable garden and behind the back shed that hid them from the windows where his mother might be watching. Usually Kenny just unfastened his fly and pulled out his dick, but this time he pulled his shorts down so she could see all of him, the raw, awkward little sprouts that were stuck on him, like something left over. His water splashed on the ground, and that made Edith aware of other sounds in the air, a distant car, a wasp under the eaves of the shed, a bird in the field behind them.

When he finished, he pulled up his shorts and wiggled them to get comfortable.

"You want to show me?" he said.

"No," Edith said, "not today."

As they walked by the garden, they ate some bitter-tasting leaf lettuce, then they returned to the cars, but Edith was tired of her story.

"I have to go now," she said.

"You can have the truck road."

"No. I have to go."

When she got home, Edith found her mother in front of the mirror in the hall, her hair brushed, and her face made up with lipstick and powder. She was putting her compact back in her purse. The pieces of the record were gone from the living-room floor.

"I'm going to your grandmother's for a few minutes," she said. "I left a sandwich, and I asked Vi to keep an eye on you, so don't go anywhere without you tell her. I'll be back before you have to go to bed."

She looked down at Edith, her eyes still swollen from crying.

"Your hands are filthy. You make sure to wash them before you eat."

The screen door slammed behind her. Edith looked at

her hands; they were dirty, from the earth at Kenny's, so she went to the kitchen to wash them. On a plate on the kitchen table was a cheese sandwich cut into quarters. Edith took a bite and then went to the sink, to wash her hands while she chewed it.

When she'd eaten the sandwich, she poured herself a glass of milk. The empty house made small noises around her. Inside the back door her father's baseball jacket hung on a nail, reminding her of the way things used to be.

The silver heart was still there in the drawer in her room. She took it out and went downstairs with it gripped in her hand. From the sideboard she took out her father's favourite record, Caruso and another man singing together. She put the heart down just long enough to put on the record, then sat with it in her hand and listened to the two voices, the melody so beautiful and yearning that you couldn't bear it to be over.

She didn't cry. Vi was wrong, she didn't need a good cry; the music was better, sadder, but infinitely more wonderful.

She played the record four times, and then, carefully, she put it away to be saved until her father returned from war.

# Chapter 6

Yesterday they had stood naked in the pouring rain, the first they had seen since they came ashore at the beach by Le Grotticelle. For two weeks they had marched forward, or ridden on the tanks and Bren carriers, and when there was a minute free they fell asleep. If they had learned nothing else, they had learned that fear was exhausting, that a mile walked at home in happiness over a familiar road was half the length of a mile walked here, in a strange country in constant fear of the German ambush that might lie in wait, the crackle of automatic weapons, the murderous eruption of a mortar attack.

Ralph was watching a small green lizard that hung on the shaded side of a dusty rock. The tiny toes of the creature gripped the stone, and it hung motionless as Ralph lay observing it in the incendiary rays of the Sicilian sun. He and the lizard stared at each other. It had the sly ancient eyes of an old bachelor. Stone eyes. It was a bright, sour green colour. Like everything here, it was older than history. As he lay there, his head in the shade of his pack, Ralph realized that the stone from which the lizard watched him had been cut square by human hands. It was a piece of some ancient ruin. They saw them everywhere in the hard hilly landscape here. Heaps of stone that had been castles or churches or houses.

He would have liked to know what kind of ruin it was. Roman, was that it? They'd had a lecture on the boat about the country they were going to invade, but the officer − swaying a little with the pitch of the boat, his voice like a tiny echo of the deep bass throbbing of the engines − had concentrated on money and language and VD and Fascism.

The Romans had been here, and who else? The Carthaginians? Ask the little green lizard with his stone eyes. He had watched them all, and to him every soldier was the same. He lived happily on the ruins they left behind.

As they fought their way across Sicily, the Canadians were leaving new ruins, hill towns pounded to bits by artillery and mortars and grenades. Leonforte: the strong lion; he had imagined it like a lion, tawny and dangerous, curled up in the sun asleep as they observed it from the river crossing. But when they had gone in, at night, hanging on the rattling tanks and guns that raced across the new bridge thrown up by the Engineers, moving at top speed to avoid the German fire from above, it was a beast of darkness, armed with sudden scatterings of hot steel that sought his death.

The lizard shifted its feet a fraction of an inch and then was still again, as if it were painted on the rock. Except the bright eyes. Ralph moved his arm slowly out from his side and in a roundabout movement through the air and toward the small green body. His hand swept down and seized it, and it wriggled and nearly escaped until he was able to immobilize it between his fingers. He turned over and held it out toward Tarleton Beamish, who lay on the ground on the other side of him. Some of the other members of the company were using their hours of freedom to write letters, but Ralph and Tart had simply dropped to earth, to sleep or at least lie still. Ralph knew he should be writing to Verna, but he found it hard to know what to say. It was easier if he imagined his daughter Edith reading the letters.

"Look," he said to Tart, "I caught one."

Tart reached out his wide hand and took the small body of the lizard.

"Ugly little shit," he said.

He held the narrow head of the lizard between his big thumb and his first finger and squeezed for a second to crush it. Then he threw down the green body and wiped his fingers in the dust.

Ralph felt a small chill as he looked at the lizard, still twitching on the earth. Death came so easily. He shouldn't have shown the small creature to Tart. He might have known what would happen.

Tart was a natural soldier. He had saved Ralph's life in Leonforte, when they were pinned down by machine-gun fire, the German mortars just about to find the range when Tart levered his way onto a tile roof, crawled across it and found an angle from which he could fire on the machine-gun crew.

Ralph reached out and scooped the dead lizard into a crack between the rocks where he didn't have to see its body. He felt lonelier now, more uneasy about the next day and the days after. There was something about being watched by those tiny cold eyes that had been almost comforting.

His fingers, where they had touched the ground, were covered with dust. Already the earth had dried after the rain of the previous day.

It was a strange sight, all those naked men soaping their bodies in the rain; the corporal, McVety, had started it, and soon the whole company had stripped down for their first good wash since they had come ashore. And now their first real rest.

Ralph lay with his head on his arm, staring across the hills to the place in the distance where the mountain, Etna, appeared like some traveller's mirage, traces of snow still showing on its top even while the country around it baked in the sun. For days the presence had been there as they moved toward it and then around it. He stared at the whiteness of the snow which reflected the bright sunlight back toward him. The square outline that pressed upward out of the rolling plains and into the sky began to shimmer, to vibrate in his eyes, and he thought of the lava that burned somewhere in the earth beneath it, ready to pour out and drown the landscape in fire and ash.

He shifted his eyes. A few feet away, young Eldwin Tyson was sitting on the ground, leaning against his pack, which he'd propped against a rock. Using the bottom of his mess tin for a kind of writing desk, he was carefully inscribing the words of a letter to his parents, his pencil pressing down on the paper as if he might be cutting into metal or stone, his boyish face concentrated on the words he was creating.

If Ralph told Verna and Edith about the volcano, would the censors pass it or would it give away information about their position? Would Verna be interested? It wasn't the kind of thing she liked; anything too unusual frightened her. When he was courting her, Ralph had always felt proudly protective because she was so easily frightened. It made her feminine and appealing. But after they were married it seemed like some kind of refusal. Too often he couldn't make her laugh or look happy. She was like the house she kept, everything neat and clean and in its place, with no surprises.

At first he'd felt guilty about the girl in England, Phyllis, but then he reflected on how far he was from home, that he might not survive the war, and the guilt went away. They were just a man and woman alone at the edge of a shattered world, and they shared laughter and warmth. Ralph tried not to make comparisons between her and Verna, but he couldn't help being aware that he didn't have to be careful all the time with Phyllis, the way he did with his wife. Maybe if he got back, he'd find that Verna had changed.

When Ralph enlisted, Alfred Bowman had told him that there would always be a job for him in his hardware and lumber business, and sometimes they had talked about expanding the rickety, low-roofed back shop where Ralph did some tinsmithing and electrical repairs – maybe even going into construction. Ralph had been eager, knowing he could do well. But all that was far away, impossible. Planning for the future was tempting fate. If he got back, Verna would be there, and things would have to work themselves out.

There was Edith too. It would soon be her tenth

birthday. He must find something to send her. Inside his paybook was the picture that Verna had sent, a snapshot Vi had taken, of the two of them standing in the backyard of the house, and he was surprised at how much taller the girl had got. She wasn't smiling in the picture, but she didn't look sulky, just serious, as if she knew that the photo would be sent to her father and was trying to concentrate in her expression something that would cross the ocean and find its way to a man in battle.

She was serious in a nice way. Last summer she went to all the softball games and wrote to tell him how the team had done without him. It was nearly two years since he had seen her. Two years, since they had left Canada for training in England.

He looked back at Mount Etna. As he stared at it, it seemed to be moving in the air.

"When do you suppose we'll get our first piece of Eyetie ass?" Tart said.

"Probably about Christmas," Ralph said.

"If I have to wait that long I'll be goin' after one of these little donkeys we're using for transport."

"Sharp hooves," Ralph said.

Tart laughed.

"Have to tie all four legs together," he said. "Like a calf in a rodeo."

The grey and white form of the volcano was still dancing in the air, but if he looked away he knew that it would stop. Tart began mumbling an obscene little rhyme that he liked to repeat over and over to himself. He'd been chanting it to himself when he went across that roof in Leonforte.

Eldwin Tyson finished his letter and folded it up. Ralph

realized that he was listening to the sounds of artillery from the lines a few miles in front of them, but listening in the way that was automatic now, like a farmer's awareness of the weather. Soldiers lived and died by sounds.

It was in Leonforte that Ralph had killed a man from close up for the first time, as they were fighting their way through the streets, from doorway to doorway. The German soldier was short, heavyset, with a round face, innocent even under the square helmet. He was running up an alley as Ralph ducked into it away from machine-gun fire; Ralph and Tart had got separated, but Ralph had the Bren, and when he came face to face with the German, he fired from the hip, and what he was most aware of as the bullets struck the man and threw him down was the repeated sound of the gun − chunk, chunk, chunk − as it leaped in his hands. He emptied the magazine into the body of the German soldier as he fell, and the final bullet hit his face and tore it open.

He could remember all the sounds of that moment, his ears ringing from a mortar shell that exploded nearby, the grinding of tank tracks on stone as one of the Shermans laboured up the hilly street, the rhythmic bursts of machine-gun fire, the pounding of a self-propelled gun a couple of streets away. It was this awareness of sound that kept you alive; if you heard what threatened you, you might avoid it. Once you had seen it, it was often too late.

The distant artillery was the sound of what was prepared for you when you went back into battle; they dropped their heavy shells on the German position − it would be a hilltop, the Germans were smart enough to choose fortified hilltops as their defence positions − and then the men of the infantry would move in. It wasn't until Leonforte he had known how bad it could be.

It was easy at first. The Italians wanted no more part of the war, and they were eager to surrender. When Ralph's company jumped out of the landing-craft and began to struggle through the water toward the beaches, it was their first confrontation with battle. They had all heard the stories about Dieppe, and they expected an inferno. But when they reached the sand and began to cross toward the wire, there was little machine-gun fire − a few bursts on their left, and by the time the wire was cut, the bewildered Italian soldiers were ready to surrender.

As they came off the beach, there was a hint of light in the sky to the east, and as they marched past the rank salt marshes that covered the low-lying area above the sand, the sky grew brighter. There was a rumble of artillery somewhere, but they couldn't tell where. Their ears hadn't yet been sharpened by the experience of battle. By the time the sun rose they were a few miles inland, near a whitewashed farmhouse. The flat walls of the house, the red-tile roof, the stone walls of the animal pens were vivid in the golden sunlight, strange and peaceful, like a picture from a magazine. As they arrived at the house, they learned that the lead company had killed an Italian soldier here.

It was all like that at first, unreal, frightening for the shapelessness of it all − a little fighting, a few deaths − but nothing that seemed like war. Even comic sometimes. There was the sergeant who captured an Italian general; the general was willing enough to surrender, but only to a senior officer, and he sat tight while the other ranks searched out an officer for him to surrender to. Yet all the time they knew that somewhere in front of them the Germans waited, real soldiers, not like these unhappy Italians.

They moved quickly inland, short of supplies, more apprehensive as they grew tired, and finally, in the hills, the real war began. For the first time Ralph saw another man over the sights of his rifle. It was a German machine-gunner, half visible in a machine-gun nest of rocks. As he aimed at him, Ralph had a sudden absurd feeling that he was back on the rifle range at Borden, the men in the bunker below the targets waving signals after each shot, the signal stick inverted for a complete miss, waved with the little metal circle up for a hit, the black circle held over the bullet's location on the target. Ralph was the best shot in the company. It was like baseball; he just had the eye for it.

He held the German in the sight, took the first pressure and drew the trigger toward him. He felt the punch of the recoil against his shoulder, and saw the German vanish behind the stones. Then there was a sudden shaking in his legs, and a kind of momentary light around everything in front of him, and then Eldwin Tyson was on his feet and running up the hill toward the German lines and Ralph jumped up and followed him.

How long ago was that? A week? Ten days? It was that night − or was it the next? − that some little Italian nuns had insisted on serving them ersatz coffee. One of them, so small she might have been a child, had attached herself to Ralph, smiling broadly at him, babbling things in Italian that he couldn't understand, bringing him a second cup of coffee. When they left, she made some kind of sign toward him that might have been a blessing.

"She was giving you the big eye, Ralphie," Tart said as they walked away.

"She's a nun."

"Don't let them fool you. My old man was a dogan, and he gave me the lowdown on nuns."

"You're full of shit, Beamish." It was Frenchie Menard who had spoken. "You don't know nothin' about the sisters. They're good women."

"You micks stick together."

"You said your father was one."

"He was too smart. He got out."

"That's smart eh?"

"Listen, he worked in Montreal once, worked with this guy, and the guy's mother died. The guy's straight dogan, good as gold. He goes to the priest and the priest won't bury her unless he pays through the nose. The guy hasn't got the money, but that's it, no money, no funeral. The guy had to beg for the money. To bury his mother."

"The guy probably had the money, he just didn't want to spend it."

The argument had gone on half the night, and from that night on, Frenchie hadn't spoken to Tart. Every time he saw Frenchie go by, Tart crossed himself, and one morning as they were leaving a village where they'd spent the night, he ostentatiously pissed against the wall of a church when Frenchie could see him and Ralph had stepped between them just in time to stop a fight.

The argument was over now. Frenchie had been blown to pieces in Leonforte by an exploding mortar shell.

She had such a kind smile, that tiny nun, but now she

was gone. Things came and went so fast in war; everyone was temporary except those left at home, and they seemed less than real. What was real was the reflex acts of fighting, the presence of the enemy, the noise. War was its own world.

The angle of sun on the mountain was different now, and the reflected light was not as bright; the volcano was still and solid, no longer a mirage dancing over the earth.

It was stone and vast. Everything around them was stone and sun, and men came here to destroy each other. And they learned, as he and Tart were learning, to stretch their luck, to be untouchable by the human shocks. The man who died by your bullets would have killed you if you hadn't shot him first. You learned to be like stone, to be unshattered by the pounding noises in your ears, the constant crash of explosions.

He tried to plan a letter to Verna, but he had no words. It was easier to think of Phyllis. That was dark and simple. That was the kind of love for soldiers. They said that they were fighting for their families at home, but that wasn't true. They fought today because they had fought yesterday. It had become their trade. As they walked toward death, they had learned to feel a strange drugged comfort that kept the fear, for now, at bay.

All around him on this Sicilian hilltop, young Canadian men in khaki sat or lay in postures of ease. In the distance they could hear the guns.

# Chapter 7

Edith sat on the edge of one of the dry fountains in the Piazza Farnese and studied the huge black building in front of her. The Farnese Palace was the French Embassy now, guarded by *carabinieri*. It was an immense building, dark and powerful, details carefully repeated with slight variation to give a sense of geometrical order. Authority. In *Tosca*, her last, lost opera, the building was the lair of the sadistic Baron Scarpia.

The Farnese Palace was a part of the City of Power, which was one of the masks of Rome and had been since the legions marched out to dominate the known world. The palace had been built, by Michelangelo and others, to express the splendour of one of the Farnese popes.

The piazza around her was crowded with parked cars, and among them, not far from her, was a trailer designed to be pulled behind a bicycle. It was a rectangular box, six feet or so long, and looked not unlike a large coffin on wheels. In front of it, a young man was cooking a meal on a camp stove. He must live in the little trailer, right here in the middle of the busy square. If he was told to move on, he could simply hitch it to his bicycle and pedal off to some new location.

A life of freedom, of a sort. Now that she had no lasting connection with the world, Edith could run away and live a life like that.

No. She was not suited for it. She liked her comfortable apartment, though she was uneasy in it these days, unable to fill the time without scores to study, hours of practice to complete.

She walked on, through the narrow streets of *vecchia Roma*. Before the recent letter (Had it really come? It couldn't have.) her last contact with her father had been a postcard sent from this city. A postcard of the Colosseum. He had vanished here, and now he threatened to reappear.

Edith stood by the piano in her apartment, reached out and pressed down a key. The note sang, and as it died away she allowed herself to hum the pitch, the sound ringing very softly in her head. Then she was silent and felt in her body an emptiness, a soft ache, an awareness of something missing. Her body needed the sensation of her voice ringing through it. Again she reached out and touched a note on the piano, then lifted her finger and let it fall into silence. She could sing that note or any other. She could let her voice free from its captivity.

On the piano was the score of *Der Rosenkavalier*. A few months before, she had begun to work on it after asking Milton and Mildred to look for a production for her. But she could not walk on stage, not any more.

She hummed quietly, then opened her mouth, letting the sound out into the room, holding a single vowel. Lovely. No. She stopped. It was over. She walked away from the piano, took down her coat and went out to exercise herself into exhaustion. She would walk to the Colosseum.

Edith set the table with a flask of white wine and a cold bottle of mineral water from the refrigerator. She put out a bowl of blood oranges, and small plates. She'd sent Nancy down to Campo de' Fiori for some cheese and fresh bread.

The lunch was unplanned, impulsive. She had been listening to the girl sing, interrupting now and then to analyse the shape of a phrase, to talk about the meaning of the words, then returning to her chair and watching the pleasant bland face, aware that she was a little hungry and asking herself why she should not invite the girl to stay for lunch with her.

Strange: it had come to her that way, as the questioning of a prohibition. All things between student and teacher were to be formal, proper, was that it? Or had she become that sort of person, old, uneasy with those younger, stiff, formal? Part of her resistance to teaching Nancy Longridge had been a dislike of intrusion, a distaste for the idea of having a stranger in her home. But with her public self lost, the performer who stood in front of thousands and touched them with her voice, with the power of her feeling, she must revise the private person to match her new situation.

A week before, somewhat to her own astonishment, she had phoned the girl and told her to come for lessons, but without her pious husband-accompanist – they would not need an accompanist at first, Edith had said. Now she had invited the girl to stay for lunch, given her a few thousand lire to walk down the alley to the shops at the edge of the market. At first the girl, who had little Italian, had looked uncomfortable about the idea, but she quickly summoned up her courage and set off. One could observe her drawing in breath, setting her head straight. Perhaps the blandness of that face was something achieved, the reflection of a refusal to flinch.

Edith wanted to known more about her. The voice itself was so beautiful, serene and pure. That was a trap, of course. Edith had known too many singers not to recognize that a beautiful voice might not reflect any splendid qualities in the personality that possessed it. One knew, did not believe, quite, ever.

Size it lacked, a little. Spaciousness. Some of that would come with age, and some with knowledge of a larger world, and some from technical achievement, more spaces in the throat and head set resonating by every note.

The buzzer summoned her, and she went eagerly, glad that the girl was back. Was she so desperate for company now that she had no performances to prepare, no travel to plan? When she opened the door, Nancy, with her bright, prepared smile, was holding flowers out to her.

"I saw them at the market," she said. "I wanted to get them for you."

"Thank you," Edith said. "*Grazie tante.*"

She took the flowers and turned to go up the stairs. The girl's gesture shocked her, made her feel naked, uneasy.

"There's been a flower market there for centuries," she said. "That's where the *campo* gets its name."

"There's so much out on the stalls," Nancy said. "I

wanted to buy it all. I was very tempted by a fish. It seemed to have its eye on me."

Who was this girl, buying flowers, joking about fish? She was not the pious, formal, empty creature Edith had invited. This was all going astray, somehow, changing.

When Edith had put the flowers in water, she set the bread and cheese on the table, alongside the oranges and a plate of olives.

"I like this part of Rome better than where we're staying," Nancy was saying. "It's more like what I imagined."

"It's a very old neighbourhood. Shall I pour you some wine?"

"Yes, a little, please."

"I only have white. Red is bad for the voice. Did anyone teach you that?"

"I don't usually drink very much."

"Red wine makes things swell up."

Edith poured a glass of wine for the young woman, one for herself.

"I still don't keep red wine. Just a superstition, I suppose, now I'm not singing any more."

"Why aren't you singing?"

Edith looked at the pale face, the blue eyes watching her intently. It seemed less bland now, less placid. She was aware of small indentations at the side of the nose that came and went with certain expressions, a pale transparent down on an upper lip that seemed to curl and grow shorter when the girl smiled or spoke. The face, from close up, was full of activity and energy. Could she tell this girl the truth? If she understood would it only frighten her?

"One reaches a certain age," she said, "when what was natural isn't natural any more."

"Everything…", the girl said in response, though there was no obvious connection, "is so different."

"Different from what?"

"From what you expect."

"You mean in Rome?"

"Everywhere."

"I don't know what you mean."

"Neither do I, I guess. I've never been very bright. Lee can explain things I can't."

"Do you agree with his explanations?"

"I like to think there's a reason for things."

"The most important things can't be explained."

"What kind of things?"

"Things like why you have such a beautiful voice."

"Lee says it's a gift of God."

"What do you think?"

"I don't have to think about it," she said. "I just sing."

"Sit down and we'll eat."

The two of them took their places.

"Did you have any trouble buying the bread and cheese?"

"Mostly I just pointed."

"You should try to learn some Italian while you're here. If you're going to sing seriously, you'll have to know it."

"My teacher in Toronto used to sound it out for me."

"That's all right up to a point, but if you're going to sing anything of any weight, you have to understand what you're singing."

"There's so much to learn."

"You could probably find some Italian who wants to

practise English and take turns speaking English and Italian."

"I guess I should."

"I assume you came to Italy and came to me to learn opera. If you want to do that, you have to learn Italian. And besides, the language is good for your voice, all the clear open vowels and big bright consonants."

"I like listening to the language when we're out on the street."

"You'll soon catch on. It's an easy language. Did you take French or Latin in school?"

"I did French for a couple of years."

"That will help you with Italian."

"I'm not sure about opera. I started out singing in church, and opera always seemed...outlandish."

"Don't you like dressing up? For Hallowe'en or a costume party?"

"I always liked Hallowe'en. Being a witch or a ghost."

"That's opera. Hallowe'en. A costume party. A different world. Magic. Half the women are whores and the other half are crazy, but when you start to pretend that you have those things inside you, you find that you do."

"You make it sound exciting and dangerous."

"It is. Very dark and very bright. I've just been reading about Puccini, things I'd forgotten about him. There's always something nasty in his operas, you know. His father died when he was young, and he was brought up as a spoiled little boy surrounded by sisters. That was flattering to him, exciting, but it was dangerous too. All these women, these strange creatures who cosseted him but also had him at their mercy. So when he grew up he had to be a conqueror. He loved shooting birds and animals. A lecher, but in his operas he loves to get sentimental over the victims of lechery. When you sing Puccini, you're embroiled in a messy affair with a self-indulgent narcissist who wants to make you suffer and then cry over you."

The girl had stopped eating. She was staring at Edith.

"How do you learn these things?" she said.

Edith laughed.

"I just make them up," she said. "Probably it's all nonsense, but once you get inside these crazy stories you have to learn to believe your own nonsense. You start to ask yourself if Tosca is really half attracted to Scarpia. You believe any crazy thing that helps you to go out on the stage and touch the audience."

Edith stopped. Something was almost out of control. The girl's intent listening, the bright open eyes, had made her say these things, made her forget that she was no longer of that world, that she was a failed and fading singer immured in her apartment in old Rome and trying to learn to be only a teacher, waiting for some man she didn't know to come and say he was her father.

"Eat," she said to the girl. "I talk too much."

It was late in the evening. They sat in Ezio's apartment. He put down the glass of Scotch he had been sipping.

"I was sure I heard you, yesterday, singing in your apartment."

"I'll have to move farther away, if you're going to spy on me."

"You know you must go back to it."

"No. I don't know that."

"If you don't know that, you know nothing."

"Singers are very stupid."

"Some are, but not Edith Fulton."

"You'd be suprised how stupid I can be, Ezio."

"Obstinate. You are only obstinate and wilful. And afraid."

"Yes, I'm afraid."

"Of the past."

"Of failure. Of humiliation."

"But you are very strong."

"I always thought so."

"You will sing again. I know it."

"For centuries men knew the earth was flat."

"The curvature of the earth is so slight that in practice, in ordinary human experience, it is flat."

"You're very adept at argument, Ezio."

"My legal training."

"You were trained in the law but you don't practise law. I was trained to sing, but I do not sing."

"There is a difference. I do not need to practise the law."

"Because you have money."

"Because it is not important to me. You need to sing."

"Yes," she found herself saying, "I do. My voice is the instrument of my soul, the only glimpse of perfection I will ever be allowed. And I will never sing again."

She walked to the door of the apartment and out into the night.

"*Bene*," Edith said, "*molto bene*."

"*Grazie*," the girl said shyly in reply.

Edith was sitting on the bench in front of her piano. She had struck only the occasional chord as Nancy sang her way through '*Ah, fors'è lui.*' She held pitch beautifully

without accompaniment. Before she let her sing it, Edith
had talked about Violetta, about Marguerite Gautier in
the Dumas novel, even about *Camille*, the old movie of
the Dumas story with Garbo and Robert Taylor — trying
to make the girl imagine the luminous beauty of Garbo's
face — and although Nancy had never seen Garbo, probably never before heard of her, Edith, looking at her as
she sang, would have sworn that she had seen a reflection of Garbo's lovely features on the young face in front of
her. More and more she realized that the blankness she
had seen on Nancy's face the day of her arrival was the
blankness of a sheet of paper on which the most remarkable poetry might be written. The girl could pick feelings
out of the air and wear them as her own.

"How's the Italian coming?" Edith said.

"I'm learning a little, I guess. Signora Farlatti isn't very
patient."

"Are you patient with her?"

"If I try to tell her she's making a mistake in her English,
she just explains to my why what she said is better."

"She'll be good training for you in not letting yourself
be bullied."

"Usually I just give up."

"Don't. Most Italians like to argue."

Nancy was looking toward her, something tentative in
her look.

"Why did you come to Italy, Edith?"

Edith thought, wondered.

"Because it was where the greatest singers came from.
Because it was distant and exotic, a long way from everything I'd grown up with. There was another reason too.
My father came here in the Second War with the Canadian Army. He never came back."

Edith's fingers reached for the piano, stroked the keys without sounding any. Would she tell the rest of the story?

"How old were you when he went away?"

"Eight."

"You never saw him after that?"

"No."

The seconds counted themselves away, and the moment when she might have told Nancy about the letter passed by like a ghost.

"You never got married."

"No."

"You chose to have a career instead."

What an odd girl this was. One minute she showed the most astonishing intuition, and the next she sounded like *Ladies' Home Journal.*

"I'm not sure I always knew what I was choosing, but the voice is a very demanding instrument."

"Yes."

Was the girl merely being agreeable? Did she understand at all?

"You have a natural gift," Edith said, "but eventually you'll have to take responsibility for its development. You'll have to decide how much of yourself you want to commit to singing. To sing seriously means to sing for an audience, and that means study and planning and bitter competition. It's a very impure world. You have to struggle to build a place where people will come and hear you. You get covered with mud and dust."

"What about children?" Nancy said. "Lee wants to have children."

"One more thing to plan. One more responsibility. It's no problem physically. Women sing beautifully when they're pregnant. If there's enough money, you can hire a nurse. You have to take it all into account. You have to ask yourself what you really want."

"I want to come here and study with you. Right now that's all I want."

Edith stood up from the piano bench.

"So for now, you're doing what you want. We won't borrow trouble."

When Nancy was gone, Edith wandered idly about her apartment, staring out windows, over the jumble of roofs. She had never married. She had chosen to have a career instead. The voice is a very demanding instrument. It's a very impure world. The words she had heard, the words she had spoken, were equally absurd. Life was activity and then staring out the window. Minute followed minute, and there were no conclusions to be drawn. Edith had built the place where people could come and hear her sing, and now she had dismantled it. It had proved to be not a stone palazzo but a jerry-built shack. A strong wind had knocked it down.

Some of her scores were piled on a table near the piano. She went and picked one up. *Le Nozze di Figaro*. The lines and dots were arbitrary, meaningless. She put it back down.

Later, she put on a coat and walked to Campo de' Fiori. Behind the black brooding statue of Giordano Bruno, a young boy was kicking a soccer ball, and each time, his mother, a heavyset woman in a brown skirt, kicked it skilfully back to him. Mother and son, kicking a ball, guarded by the statue of a martyr to freedom of thought.

# Chapter 8

*Sorry her lot who loves too well,*
*Heavy the heart that hopes but vainly.*

As she sang, the notes fluttering in her throat like a winged thing, she felt the eyes in front of her in the darkness of the school auditorium. Now and then, even blinded as she was by the spotlight from the back and the brightness that came at her from the sides and above, and below, she would see movement in the auditorium, huddled shapes that scurried together to confer, Miss Chambers the costume mistress being questioned by Mr Hollett the director, or Mr Reeves, whose shop class had built the set, conferring with Miss Ingle, whose art class had painted it.

But the movements out there were at a tangent, unconnected, random. The lights cut her off from those tiny facts, those shadows of a half-world that found its focus in her, her voice floating over the chords that Penny Esford dutifully and accurately pressed out of the piano. The triple time of the music gently held her body in its wavering beat, and when she lilted across the stage it was movement perfected, her legs lightened by the stir of the music's beat, the long skirt of her dress just caressing the floor with the sibilant sound that had startled her when she entered in costume, alone and silent, while the teachers below conferred on the fit and design of the dress. She had crossed the blank cavern and spun round to face them, and at first the hem had hissed slightly; then, as she turned, it lifted away from the wood and was silent.

Was he there in the darkness? She had seen the lighted windows of Room 212, the history room, his room – with its yellowed maps and the one glassed-in shelf of books, the bust of Napoleon – as she arrived at the front door of the school, an apparently accidental glance carrying her eyes upward. As always. She had no way of being sure whether he was in the room, working late, or whether it was only the caretaker.

*Sad are the sighs that own the spell*
*Uttered by eyes that speak too plainly.*

Perhaps he was in the darkness of the auditorium, observing her, listening to the words. Would not like them, the softness of their aspiration, their sentiment. Be hard, he always said, be hard and shining. More likely, he was in his room, bent over the desk, his face a little pale in the barren light of the schoolroom, at work, unaware that she was in the building, unaware of the words that she was singing.

He did notice her; she knew it. In class, she would look up and be aware that his eyes had flickered away just as hers had risen to catch them. She was sure. Sometimes.

Other times, she was afraid she was creating it all, out of whole cloth, a foolish schoolgirl fantasy. If only there were someone she could tell. Someone wise and astute. But there was no one. Her mother would be scathing; little girls making eyes at teachers, who was Edith to think such a man would be interested in her? Her mother who went to the movies with Sid Appleton every Saturday and invited him to dinner every Sunday, and waited, apparently, for him to propose marriage. Edith had sworn to herself that if that unlikely miracle should ever happen, she would move out before Sid moved in. He was so slow, so heavy. Ponderous was the word Edith had chosen for him. Ponderous.

Edith had a few friends, but she knew them to be shallow, complacent girls, good enough company, and a helpful source of the gossip which was a substantial part of her education in sexual matters, but not to be confronted with the complicated questions and feelings involved in this case. They already thought her odd, eccentric. It would become, flatly, a "crush." *Edith has a crush on Mr Lannan.* And each of the others, Bonnie and Liz and Marg, would reciprocate with a secret crush on some other teacher, and the conversation would devolve into a stew of gossipy questions: Did Miss Chambers really touch the girls too much when she was trying on their costumes? Should Bonnie let Phil put his fingers inside her bra? Edith didn't mind these sessions; there was a giddy, feverish excitement to them. Her face and body would flush; she would feel naked, daring, crazily exposed.

Yet that was the ordinary world, suitable for discussion as to whether she would go to the cast party with Martin Klassen, who played Ralph Rackstraw, and whether they would extend their chaste on-stage love-making into something more. Martin was all right; she wouldn't mind kissing him in a secret corner, pressing against him, but she wouldn't take it seriously.

David Lannan. She hardly let herself know his given name, teachers' first names were a part of the joking irreverence of students rebelling against the decorum of school. Stale and cheap. It was all so impossible, in so many ways; she was surrounded by, threatened by, the complacencies, the desperate ordinariness of the school, the town, the whole world, it sometimes seemed. He stood for rarity. He didn't pander to his student with jokes. Be hard, he had said to her, you must be hard and shining; he included her in the world of brilliant possibilities. It was for that she loved him.

Love. Loved. She must not say it, nor even think it. It was too dangerous. She was too proud to fall into such vulgarity.

*Sad is the hour when sets the sun,*
*Dark is the night to earth's poor daughters,*
*When to the ark the wearied one*
*Flies from the empty waste of waters.*

The words caught the pain of her solitude, that she could not speak aloud what was most central to her life, for the very mention of it would make it false. Yet she treasured the loneliness; he had often spoken of the essential solitude of all human heroism; Caesar was alone, Alexander was alone, Napoleon was alone. The others around them never understood the quality of the world they were creating in their minds. Somehow, in childhood, each had learned that he was different, that he possessed a uniqueness, a special quality, that he dreamed strange dreams.

Edith had always been proudly alone, secretly freakish, a monster in disguise. Perhaps if her father had come back from the war it would have been different. It was growing harder to remember him, but she still treasured the silver heart he had given her, and the scratchy old records. Sometimes when she was alone in the house, she would go into the bathroom and listen to the echo of her voice when she sang, then put on one of the recordings of Emma Eames or Marcella Sembrich, and try to compare the sound. Or she would sing with them, imitating the Italian sounds she didn't understand. Once her mother had come in and caught her at it, said nothing, only looked at her as if she were some kind of insect, who, if she were ignored, might disappear down a crack in the floor.

Tomorrow would be her revenge. There would be hundreds of people in the auditorium, and Edith would be safe and brilliant in the make-up and costume, and her voice would make them listen and marvel.

*Heavy the sorrow that bows the head*
*When love is alive and hope is dead.*

Edith breathed deeply and prepared for the final run up to a high B flat. She knew the note was sometimes shrill, and Mr Esford had suggested that he could rewrite the music to go only as high as G, but Edith insisted. There was no one else in the cast — perhaps no one else in town — who could sing a high B flat that wasn't a mere squeal, and if she didn't try to hold it too long it would be brilliant and startling. She wanted to astonish them all. None of them had so much as heard of Galli Curci or Emma Eames or even Lily Pons. David Lannan knew of them – he seemed to have read everything, to know everything – but he had no real interest in music, and would perhaps not even come to a performance. She hoped he might look in tonight, just long enough to see her on the stage, to hear a few notes, even if he concluded that she was vain and frivolous and *H.M.S. Pinafore* a foolish trifle. Was he there in the dark? Did he care that the dress was flattering to her, made her shape fuller and more elegant?

*When love is alive and hope is dead.*

Her voice ran up to the B flat and down to the last note. From the auditorium there was a little applause, a few of the invisible watchers clapping their hands in the empty room.

The next day some of the members of the cast stayed home from school; although it wasn't officially permitted, no one would make a fuss. But Edith spent the day at school. A day at home would have provoked comment from her mother, that Edith was self-important, inflated with the significance of her first appearance on stage. Also she had a history class, and she knew that Mr Lannan would disapprove of an unnecessary absence. He would regard it as a weakness, a self-indulgence. Odd: Mr Lannan and her mother would reach similar conclusions, which were really wholly unlike: her mother wished Edith to be ordinary; she liked her best when she was unremarkable, a flat symbolic figure: daughter. She wished to make her smaller. He, her teacher, her inspiration, wished to make her look higher, be something greater. Though he never talked about her future as some of the teachers did. Whether she would attend university. What she might study. Mr Esford, her music teacher, knew that she didn't have the money for university and was inquiring about bursaries on her behalf. She was grateful to him, and yet all of it seemed abstract, distant, a story told about someone else.

Mr Lannan's power was immediate, a flavour of possibilities in the present, a challenge. He was not especially kind to her. If she came to his room after school, his grey eyes would meet hers, he would be silent, fearfully silent. She would force herself to form coherent words, to ask a question, challenge something he had said in class. His response would be measured, thoughtful, when what she wanted was to hear something personal from him, what he thought of her, what he ate for breakfast even, knowing all the while he would be disdainful of her hunger for these merely personal things. But she had found the location of the small house where he lived, alone, and had walked past it one night. In class, he talked of the lack of rigour of those historians and biographers who thought that mere gossip was legitimate material for recording.

However nervous she was about the evening's performance, once she was in his class she forgot her worries. For a few minutes he had talked, indirectly, about himself. During the war he had served in the Intelligence Corps, and he used his own experience to illustrate certain tactical and strategic matters during Napoleon's Russian campaign.

They had been following Napoleon from his early victories, and they all knew that the campaign into Russia was to be the turning-point. These weeks of classes on the Napoleonic period were the highlight of the Grade 13 history course. Each day brought a new scene in the tremendous drama that began with the challenge of a European continent torn between aristocratic decadence and revolutionary anarchy. At the beginning of the first class on Napoleon, there was a sentence written on the blackboard.

*Napoleon Bonaparte came very near the re-establishment of our civilisation, the fixing of it permanently in a renovated, stable and noble form.*

The quotation came from a biography by Hilaire Belloc.

From the moment of reading that sentence, the students knew that the stakes were high in these events, that this was the history of human greatness. In one class after another, they had been shown the rising curve of Napoleon's fortunes, the quickness and originality of his conceptions, the clarity of his thought, the bravery of his actions.

Now he was in Moscow, and the city was burning. The governor, Rostopchin, had sent out convicts to set it alight. Winter was coming. *A Roman would have turned back*; the line spoken by someone as Napoleon reconnoitred at the bank of the river Niemen, deciding whether to advance into Russia. A Roman would have turned back. Napoleon had gone on. He had reached Moscow, and the Russians, unable to defend the city, had denied it to him by setting it on fire. Mystics, fools and saints, half mad, men of another world, the Russians could not be made to come to terms. The Tsar had sworn that he would grow his beard and eat potatoes like a peasant before he would give up a foot of his land, and the shining idea of Napoleon could not penetrate such darkness.

Edith stared, could not stop staring at the man who was telling her these things, preparing her for the destruction of the Grande Armée, the beginning of the end of the Napoleonic idea. He was a short man, with small, rounded hands, thin straight hair, a rather pale face, level grey eyes.

In front of her, Paul McDonald had his hand up. Edith resented his interruption of the flow of the story, and she knew Paul did it on purpose. He was uneasy with David Lannan's intensity, liked teachers who were friendly, joky, pretended not to take their work too seriously. The man at the front of the classroom looked toward him, ended a sentence and nodded.

"Sir, they didn't burn all of it, did they?"

"Most. Not all."

"Didn't it ever occur to Napoleon just to hang around Moscow and have a good time?"

"A good time?"

"Get in some girls and have a party."

There was a silence for a moment. The teacher stared at the boy. He knew what was expected, they all did, a joke to put him in his place, about his idea of a good time or what kind of a general he would make. The teacher didn't smile or raise his eyebrows in theatrical despair. The white soft hands came to rest on the desk in front of him. His voice remained level.

"When Napoleon wanted a woman," the man said, "he summoned the one he wanted to his tent. He told her to undress and lie down, and he continued working while she did so. And when he was finished with her, he sent her away and returned to the task at hand."

Silence hung in the air, like the silence of the burnt streets of Moscow. Edith wondered if he had gone too far, if someone would blab to parents or the principal. Teachers didn't say things like that, not in class.

"It never works when I try it," said a voice from the back, and suddenly the silence was broken by laughter, and in the middle of the laughter the bell rang for the end of the class. As Edith packed up her notebook and piled the texts on top of it, she could sense that Mr Lannan was looking at her. The laughter of the class had betrayed him, betrayed the fineness of his vision; perhaps he wished to know if she had joined that betrayal. She picked up her books and walked to the front, and just as she was passing him she stopped and looked up, and pressing her books hard against her breasts, as if to steady herself, she met his eyes.

"I'm sorry you got interrupted," she said. "It was... important, what you were saying."

She was afraid that he would look away, or merely wish her good luck on her performance, but he said nothing, only nodded a little, and she broke off the locked gaze of their eyes and left the classroom.

Edith looked out the window of her room. Sid was making his way, his *ponderous* way, along the sidewalk toward the house. As part of the evening's entertainment, he was being given a dinner of roast beef, payment perhaps for taking Verna to the high-school Gilbert and Sullivan. Probably he would have preferred a few hands of euchre. He didn't even like movies much. *H.M.S. Pinafore* would put him to sleep.

She couldn't imagine Sid and her mother naked

together. Well, probably there was no need to imagine it;
Edith felt convinced it never happened, and she suspected
that one of Sid's virtues, for Verna, was that he didn't try
to talk her into it. That was the phrase she used when she
made her one attempt at sex education for Edith. Just
don't let any boy talk you into it, because some of them
will try.

A good meal and a few hands of euchre and Sid was
satisfied. Or so it seemed.

It offended Edith that her mother had settled for
someone like Sid. Everything she could learn or remember about her father showed him as a man with something
remarkable about him; even now, if she went into the
hardware store, old Mr Bowman would have something
to say about him, how he'd just been remembering a
practical joke that Ralph had pulled on him, how Ralph
had stopped a man who was kicking a stray dog. On her
dressing-table, Edith had a picture of the championship
softball team her father had played on the summer
before he enlisted. Imagine Sid playing baseball. Or
paying two dollars for a pile of old opera records, even
though he didn't know much about opera, just thought
he might like it. If somebody asked Sid about opera, and
he didn't know the answer, would he stop off at the
library and get the librarian to look it up? That was what
her father always did if she asked him a question.

Ordinary. Verna liked things to be ordinary. She would
have found Edith's passion for David Lannan incomprehensible. Insane. Probably she had found Ralph Fulton
exasperating. Her own parents were a placid taciturn
couple who did everything in a slow orderly fashion.
That was what Verna grew up with, what she preferred,

and the accident of being born pretty — even at her most irritable Edith couldn't deny that her mother was a pretty woman, prettier than Edith would ever be — had made her seem more interesting than she was, had caused Ralph Fulton to court and marry her.

Edith looked in the mirror; she was wearing her best dress, red with a gathered waist held by a patent-leather belt, for the party after the performance. It looked all right, but not as exciting as the dress Miss Chambers had made for her to wear on stage, pale blue, almost daringly tight over her breasts, then draped at the hips and hanging elegantly to the floor.

Downstairs she heard her mother's voice. Sid spoke so quietly that she couldn't hear his responses.

When Edith got downstairs, she saw that there were three places set at the table.

"I can't eat, Mother. I'm too nervous. I had a sandwich after school."

"Of course you have to eat."

"I can't."

"Listen to that, Sid. Isn't that the limit?"

"Maybe you could eat a little," Sid mumbled. He didn't want to take sides.

"Mother, I can't eat. Do you want me to go out and throw up all over the stage?"

"Edith!"

"Well, I would."

"Faint from hunger, more likely."

"I had a sandwich after school."

"This is an expensive roast of beef."

"You and Sid eat it. I'll take it in sandwiches for lunch."

"I don't know why you think it's beneath you to have a little dinner with us."

"I'm too nervous. I have to sing."

"Listen to that, Sid."

The second appeal to Sid rankled. Edith was ready to say something cruel, but they were interrupted by a knock on the door. Her mother went to answer. It was Vi, with a ratty old coat she used for yard work thrown over her shoulders.

"I just had to come over," Vi said, "and wish Edith good luck."

"She won't even eat her dinner."

"How could she, Verna? She must be too excited." She turned to Edith. "All set?"

"I hope so." She went to Vi and hugged the big solid figure, grateful to her for being on her side.

"Mabel and I will be there cheering you on. We'll clap real loud."

"Only if I deserve it."

"Of course you will. Even when you were a little thing singing at the piano with me you had a pretty voice."

"Thanks, Vi. I'll do my best."

"You give them what for. Knock them all on their ears."

Vi hugged her again and opened the door. When she was gone, there was an emptiness, the interrupted argument still imminent, ready to start again. Edith reached to the coat rack and took her coat.

"It's time to go now," she said. At the end of the hall she could see Sid looking toward her, something unutterably sad about his wide face. There was something she ought to say to him, but she didn't know what it was.

"I wish you'd eat," her mother said.

"I'll have something after."

She pulled on her gloves and opened the door.

"Good luck," her mother said, drily, as if the words hurt.

The street outside was empty and cold. There had been a warm spell that melted much of the snow, but now everything was frozen hard again. Edith walked quickly to warm herself, the heels of her shoes knocking on the pavement. No other sound. In her head, music began, Caruso and the baritone Mario Ancona singing *"Del tempio al limitar"* from Bizet's *The Pearl Fishers*. She had played it that afternoon before Verna got back from work, played it repeatedly, as she did sometimes to try to invoke the memory of her father, his presence. That was what she had of him, a silver pendant, a photograph and the painful beauty of a record. Well, that was better than nothing, and she never tired of the music.

David Lannan wouldn't come for the performance. He found music empty, senseless. But perhaps he would look in, from the back, long enough to see her. She wanted to be seen by him; the thought roused her. If he ever...well, she knew she would, eagerly, without question.

Edith hummed to herself, just to make sure that her voice was there, that it hadn't disappeared. Her mind began to evoke all the things that could go wrong, but she tried to set them aside. She walked faster.

Outside the school, she glanced up, as always. There was a light in Room 212.

Once she was in the building, it was as if she'd boarded a fast train occupied by a circus. Everything was in motion and loud. Costumes, make-up, the jokes and preparations and good wishes of other cast members. The school had never before seemed so alive. From the room where they waited to go on stage, having their faces painted, their hair combed, they could hear the crowd arriving. Martin Klassen told her she looked pretty in her costume, and she said he looked handsome in his. The most awkward children in the cast suddenly had a fine formality about them.

The room was vibrant, all the senses assaulted, the sound of voices, jabbering, humming, giggling, the smell of cold cream and the theatrical make-up, heavy and foreign, the vivid repeated colours of the costumes, the boys dressed in identical sailor suits passing back and forth until it was like some optical illusion, a dozen figures, then none, then a dozen. Ross Petch, who was playing Sir Joseph Porter, wanted a moustache, but the make-up girls said it was too late to give him one.

Edith drew into herself, suddenly apart from what surrounded her. The thought of the stage, the audience, chilled her, and she was still and frozen. She couldn't move. Did not exist.

The room was quiet, and through the door to the stage, they could hear Penny Esford playing "God Save The Queen" and the voices of the audience following along, a shapeless whispering and rumbling sound. The boys had filed on stage for the opening chorus, and now, whenever anyone spoke, gestures from all over the room, a peremptory pantomime, would command silence.

Edith sat still, half hearing the songs and action from the stage; on the desk in front of her was a mirror, situated so that if she looked toward it she saw a corner of her face, one eye — hazel they called it, meaning no particular colour at all – with lines drawn round it so that it looked like the eye of some repellent tropical bird. She was ridiculous. When she walked on the stage, they would laugh. Mr Esford had warned her that singing on stage in front of an audience might feel strange at first, that she wouldn't recognize the feeling of her voice, but she knew now it would be worse. She would open her mouth and make the croaking sounds of a parrot, and the laughter of the audience would drive her off. She would have to quit school and leave town.

Someone was waving to her. It was time to go on. She made her way through the little door into the dark wings and saw, under the lights, the two figures of the Captain and Little Buttercup, as if they were painted figures on a china plate, the Captain, her father, all blue and white and silver, Buttercup, a fat plum in yellow. They sang the familiar words and it was her moment to enter; she tried to think of Josephine, in love with a man she could never possess, beautiful, sad. She was moving across the stage, unable for a moment to catch the sound of the accompaniment, then hearing it, grateful for the number of times Mr Esford and Mr Hollett had made her repeat this entrance and the opening of the song, for she was moving now without thinking, shocked as she turned and discovered that she could see the intent faces in the first three rows, quickly raising her eyes to look into the anonymous blackness.

> *Sorry her lot who loves too well,*
> *Heavy the heart that hopes but vainly,*
> *Sad are the sighs that own the spell*
> *Uttered by eyes that speak too plainly.*

Truly, her voice did feel odd, but gradually she came to be at home with it, to feel that she could trust it, that the music was somewhere in her body to be drawn out and hung shimmering in the air. And as she rose to the B flat, her voice was freer than ever before.

The applause startled her. It was so loud. It came at her like a great blast of wind, and it didn't stop. Hundreds of people were applauding her. She almost forgot where she was, what she was to do next, but Bill Laforge, who played her father, made his entrance and the scene went on, somehow, on its own. She was back on the fast train, everything racing past her, words, tunes, movements, until she was listening to the rising dotted notes that introduced "Refrain, audacious tar" and she was singing it, full of scorn for Ralph Rackstraw, and then, with the second melody, suddenly full of longing. She watched and listened as Ralph sang his half of the duet, rewritten by Mr Esford so that it didn't take him above F, and Martin handled it well. Under the stage lights, he did look handsome in his make-up and costume; in the next scene she would confess her love for him.

The act was over, ending in enthusiastic applause, everyone in the cast giddy now, talking thirteen to the dozen, giggling over mistakes, full of pleasure at the audience's laughter. Then it was the second act, and then that too was gone. Curtain calls, Edith feeling her face flushed with pleasure at the resonant beating of hands that acclaimed them all.

In the classroom where they were to leave props and take off their make-up, Mr Esford came to Edith and shook her hand, without saying a word, just smiled and nodded and shook her hand, and she thought for a moment she might cry. But didn't. Though she talked to those around her, laughed with them, congratulated everyone, she had gone somewhere deep inside herself, a new place, perhaps one that had never existed before, certainly never been found, a wide, spacious room, full of light.

Family members began to arrive, pleased and awkward, almost shamefaced at their own pride in the talent shown by these grown-up children. Edith saw Vi at the door of the room, waving her over, and when she went, saw Mabel and her mother a step back, Sid waiting down the hall.

"You were…" Vi said. "You…you were…"

She was shaking Edith by the shoulders, as if to shake out of her the word she was looking for.

"You were…" she said again and shook her.

"Magnificent," Mabel said quietly, if only to save Edith from being shaken to bits by Vi's inarticulate energy.

"Magnificent…no, better than that," Vi said. She hugged Edith to her.

"Don't hurt the poor girl, Violet," Mabel said.

Vi let go of her. Edith's eyes met her mother's. Verna looked away, toward Mabel.

"She was very good," Verna said. "Edith sang very well. They all did."

"You made us proud, Edith," Mabel said.

Edith looked at her mother.

"Everyone did very well," her mother said.

"There's a party," Edith said.

"Don't stay too late. And make sure they drive you home."

"And have a good time, kid," Vi said. "You going with that good-looking boy you were singing with?"

"Maybe," Edith said.

Vi nodded enthusiastically.

"We'd better let you get changed," Verna said.

"Take off the grease-paint," Vi said. "You were…" She shook Edith again.

"Magnificent," Mabel said.

They drifted away, down the wide hall toward the corner where Sid stood patiently waiting, and Edith turned back into the classroom. Someone's mother stopped her to offer congratulations. Edith thanked her and went on her way.

In front of the mirror, she studied her face as she covered it with cold cream and rubbed off the make-up on several Kleenex. There were a couple of pimples coming on her forehead. Her skin was shiny with cold cream and she wiped it again. Then her face looked white and bare, empty somehow.

Everything was different now, as if what had happened on the stage had taken her to a new place, yet left her there lost, mapless, ignorant. Sounds were abrupt and shallow; everything bright and yet flat, brittle. Vivid, but out of step. Outside the window of the schoolroom, she could see the lights of houses, and it was unbelievable, shocking, that people lived there, went about their business, slept and woke, ate, went out to work. And beyond this city others, fields, factories, a whole world. The sounds around her rasped in her ear, and yet at the same time everything she saw was part of a silent movie, inexplicable, awaiting the title card to create comprehension.

She went to the dressing-room to change. One of the girls was showing off, doing a rhumba in her bra and panties, the others giggling, one or two chastely ignoring her. As she spun and wiggled, Edith was aware of a little crease in the flesh at the top of the girl's thigh, aware of it as if it might be a medical anomaly, or a feature of a landscape studied in geography. This was the flesh of a girl, soft, smooth, delicately creased. A man might wish to touch this; any man might wish to; and perhaps her flesh was like this too, with just such a crease at the top of her thighs.

Edith went behind a screen and changed, took a comb out of her purse and drew it through her hair, looked in the mirror and combed the short waved hair into place around her skull.

"Here's the star," a little girl from the chorus said greedily as Edith came back into the crowd. The half-naked girl had finished her dance, covered herself. Everyone was dressed now, primping to be ready for the party where nothing would happen that had not happened at a thousand parties before. Edith walked out of the room and down the hall, away from the lights of the auditorium, along the high dim halls that seemed hung with a curtain of unremembered events from the past. Vi had gone to school here, and Mabel, and Ralph and Verna. The building endured all this passing of young people, all the longings and foolishness; it grew a little older, a little dingier, and yet it was essentially the same as ever. Untouched. Tonight Vi would be excited for her, some silly little girl would call her "the star," and nothing would be changed. Except perhaps within her, and who would ever know that?

On the half-lit walls were the shapes of pipes and radiators, lockers, a few pictures. Shapes.

The room was lit still. His room. She had found it by a deliberate accident. And just as she reached it, he was coming out the door. He looked at her, those level grey eyes.

"I was restless," she said. "After the performance. I was just walking around a little."

"I was on my way upstairs," he said.

Across the hall from his room was the enclosed stairway that led to the school attic where the cadet uniforms were stored, along with the Bren guns and rifles that members of the cadet corps used. He was one of the supervisors of the cadet corps; that was something foreign about him, incomprehensible.

"Have you ever been up there?"

"No."

He went and unlocked the door and opened it, flicked a switch and waited for her to enter. She had seen the boys of the school lined up here every spring, each coming out with a heavy khaki uniform over his arm; it was one of the events that punctuated the school year.

The stairway was long; steep steps with the paint worn off and the wood rubbed smooth. At the top, some kind of dark space. She began to mount the stairs, and heard the door close behind her.

It was an unimagined place she was going to, one she never thought of, except at that one moment of the year when the uniforms were brought out, and the boys of the school spent all their gym classes marching. As she listened to her feet on the stairs and his behind her, she imagined that there might be something unknown and unexpected at the top of the stairs; something out of a movie, the hidden apartment where the spy would keep his radio.

The hanging bulb at the top left most of the room in shadow. The roof sloped down on both sides and in the low areas under the slope were racks of uniforms, one after another, hung side by side like a ghost army. The bodies had gone somewhere else. The soldiers of Napoleon's squadrons vanished in the snow on the return from Moscow. Caesar's lost legions. The men killed in the war. Regiments of ghost soldiers.

He was standing beside her. It was quiet up here, and a whole world had vanished – her singing, the applause, the laughter of the others – now she was someone else, somewhere else.

"Those are the Bren guns," he said, and pointed to a pile of long rectangular black boxes straight ahead. Above them were racks of rifles.

"You came looking for me," he said.

"Yes, I guess I did."

"Weren't they all flattering you? Telling you you're wonderful?"

"Some of them."

"Then why did you come looking for me?"

"I don't know."

"Because flattery isn't nourishing. It's just a kind of emptiness. You're clever enough to know that."

"Yes," she said. "You think it's what you wanted, but it isn't."

"I never flatter you. The real rewards come from discipline and clarity."

"You make me feel that. You expect something of me. It makes me feel different. Stronger."

"People expect comfort. But it's impossible if you see things as they are."

"I know."

"No one will ever understand what it's like for you. No one will ever know what's in your mind. No one can know."

"No one? Ever?"

"What do you think? That it's like some sentimental novel?"

"No."

"I've taught you better than that."

"That's why I came to see you."

"You have some idea of how we have to create our own world."

'Yes."

"All you can ask is to be cold and alone and to see clearly."

They were silent for a moment. The cool air was rank with the dust and mould, a sharp acerbic scent in her nostrils. She was shivering.

"I knew you'd come," he said. "That flattery wouldn't be enough for you."

"I'm glad. That I came."

He was touching her face, and she was almost faint with the shock of it.

"Do you think you're strong enough?" he said.

"Yes."

Edith could hear the wind against the roof.

"I wish you liked music," she said.

"I admire Beethoven," he said, "his heroism."

"Did you hear me sing?"

"No. There was no need. I knew you'd do it well enough."

Edith felt warmed, grateful, that he expected only the best of her. That his hands would touch her. She met his eyes, waiting.

In front of one of the racks of uniforms was a low pile of canvas mats, with buttons to hold the stuffing in place, like huge lost pieces of upholstery.

"You could take off your clothes," he said.

Edith took a breath of cold air, held it.

"Or don't you want to?"

She began to undress, and as she did he went to a long table at one side of the room and set down some pieces of paper he had been carrying. Somehow she hadn't noticed them in his hands. He had been coming up here with work to do. Edith laid her dress carefully over the rail at the side of the stairwell, the crinoline beside it. When he turned back toward her, she was unfastening her stockings from the garters that held them up. He watched her as she put the stockings on top of the dress and crinoline, and then he laid aside his jacket and with those small round hands loosened his tie. As she took off the rest of her clothes, fearful and yet defiant as well, she began to shiver and couldn't stop. She made her way to the mats and lay down on top of them. In the halls of the school beneath them, the students from the cast of the opera were putting on their coats, arranging rides to the party. She couldn't quite tell if what she felt for that commonplace world down there was envy or contempt.

He switched out the light. She listened to the wind, the

soft clicks and groans of the building, the sound of the man taking off his clothes, the squeak of a floorboard as he walked toward her, and she tried to prepare herself for him, though she didn't know how, could only try to guess how she ought to lie, to open herself. His penis was harder than she expected, hurt more, but she kept silent. He held himself above her and thrust fiercely into her body.

Cold and alone. He said she must be cold and alone.

She had never been so cold and alone before.

The air was warm and lightly perfumed by the new grass and the leaves, which were just beginning to unfold. The trees along the sidewalk were familiar solid presences, had grown here all her life long, and the lights in the houses were the same lights she had seen for eighteen years; often she knew whether the front curtains would be open or closed, and sometimes she knew who lived inside; the big brick with the turret belonged to Mr Aidney, who owned the dry-goods store on the main street; the yellow brick on the corner was where the new bank manager lived. Edith told herself these things as if they were a story, a familiar story that would bring comfort, like reading *The Secret Garden* or *Anne of Green Gables* for the tenth time. The small frame house belonged to Helen Carmichael, who worked in Aidney's Dry Goods and lived alone since her father, who was odd and couldn't be let out alone, had died.

There was no comfort. For weeks now she had attended at her life as she might at a party of strangers in a distant city, every word and gesture false, produced by an effort of will, an ordinary conversation exhausting because nothing in it was spontaneous, so that by the end of the day, she could do nothing but lie on her bed and stare into the darkness. She did no schoolwork, and lying about that was as easy as lying about everything else. If she was asked to translate in Latin class, she would tell Miss Turpin that she had forgotten to prepare Virgil, thought they were still on Catullus. In every class she had some lie, some excuse. For the first time, she was grateful that most of living was so superficial; it made the pretence easier. She even thought perhaps her mother liked her better, had heard her saying to Sid that Edith had settled down now that the operetta was over. "Got it out of her system": that was the phrase she would have used.

Edith stopped in the darkness, leaned against a tree, dizzy and nauseous. That phrase: got it out of her system. Got it out of her system. Everything inside her rebelled, prepared for some huge violent vomiting that would empty her.

Nothing would empty her. There was a child growing, she swore she could see the little bulge now, and it would swell inside until she waddled and had a belly as big as a watermelon. Nothing would make that go away. She wouldn't get it out of her system. Well, she'd heard of things, something with coathangers, some dangerous violence to her insides, but that was a city thing, and too horrible to think of.

At church last year, they took up a collection for a home for unwed mothers. She hadn't needed then to ask for an address.

Perhaps he would know. He would have some idea. It was tonight she would tell him, but hated to; it was a contradiction of everything he meant to her, this burden, this heavy thing, this pregnant girl that she had become. His attitude to her had shown no change after the night of the operetta. He had been hard and demanding, as he always was, offered her no privileges except the awareness that she had his full attention, that he expected something of her. She had been hurt and bitter sometimes, as she lay in bed at night, but she remembered how he told her to expect no comfort. He had not lied.

That she might become pregnant had never occurred to her until she realized that her period was late. It was as if David Lannan belonged to some other world where the inexorable traps of biology had no power. As if the seed he had spilled inside her, that had been wet on her skin, was some spiritual secretion, something chemically alien from all other sperm, a rare substance that was immune to the simple biological fate that locked men and women into the destiny of breeding animals. When she was sure her period was late, she went to the library, thinking how many frightened girls must have done this before, pretending to be browsing over the shelves of books, glancing at this and that in the encyclopaedia, searching for something that would make her sure. She made a second trip, a third, certain that the ancient spinster librarian knew what she was seeking. The little she learned increased her fear without offering her any certainty.

She thought of consulting a doctor, a nurse, but the town was too small; such a thing could not be done in secret, and she would not see herself exposed, shamed. Edith Fulton, who had been so proud, who had stood up on stage and accepted their applause; they would love to see her brought low.

So she waited, became aware of the nausea, the undeniable knowledge that something in her body was changing, was out of her power. She had missed a second period by now. There could be no doubt; a child was growing in her abdomen; she had been taken over by another being, some alien existence that demanded the use of her blood and breath.

Her first plan was to run away. To disappear. She had enough cash to get a bus to Toronto and keep herself for a couple of weeks while she found a job. She would go to someone there, some stranger, and ask for help. There were places for girls in her condition.

In trouble.

Up the stump.

Knocked up.

She savoured the humiliating phrases. To look at it that way made it almost easier to bear.

You're up the stump, Edith Fulton. You're going to have a baby. But not here, where Verna would triumph in Edith's failure, the final proof that her proud daughter was nothing special. Vi would weep sympathetically, and that would be as bad.

They would never know. She would run away, bear the child, give up it for adoption. No one would ever know.

Unless he wanted the child.

Wanted her.

She could not imagine it, that she might stay, that she might be married to David Lannan, share a life with him. He was a stranger. Though he had torn her open, and visited the innermost privacies of her being, though he made her world vivid, she didn't know him. She could not call him by his first name.

David and Edith Lannan.

She had seen girls write their names like that in schoolbooks, joined to the names of the boys they were infatuated with, a way of imagining marriage, making the impossible real. It had always seemed to her so cheap. She did not do such things. She did not.

For a long time now, she had known that there were only two choices, to leave town, vanish, not to return, or to tell him. In class, she would look at him as he taught, wanting him to guess, to speak to her, but he never did, except about academic matters, to suggest that she write an essay on a certain aspect of the *Code Napoléon*.

Edith stood still, under a large maple tree, a block from the lights of the main street. Ahead of her, she could see the phone booth outside Seaver's drugstore; she'd phone from there. Three boys were standing on the corner across from the drugtore, one of them leaning against the wall as if he might stay there all night. She turned to walk around the block in the hope that by the time she'd done that they would have moved.

She recited the phone number to herself. She would not forget it. She was not some dimwit Ophelia. No. If they were there when she came back, she would phone all the same. It must be done and would be done.

She looked in the window of a house just as the woman inside drew down the blind.

A car moved along the street toward her. She drew her jacket tight at her throat and turned her head away. For a moment she was revealed in the headlights of the car, then it was past. It was one of the odd-looking new Studebakers. There were only a handful in town. Her father's old friend Morry Truscott owned one of them. It would be bad luck if it was Morry's car and he had recognized her. If so, he was sure to come back and offer her a ride.

The car didn't return.

When she reached the main street again, the boys were gone, and she almost ran to the phone booth, dropped in her coin, dialled. It was only a year since they'd got dial phones. A year ago she would have been forced to ask the operator for his number and risk the possibility that the woman, if she were bored that night, might listen in on the call.

She heard his voice, and for the first moment she couldn't speak.

"This is Edith Fulton," she said. She thought her strained voice must be unrecognizable. "I need to come and see you."

"After school tomorrow?"

He wasn't helping her.

"No," she said. "Tonight."

For a moment there was no sound but the soft buzzing of the phone connection.

"Yes," he said then, "of course." He said it as if he had just discovered something pleasant, a nice little surprise.

"You know where I live," he said.

"Yes."

"I'll leave the door open. Just come right in."

"All right," she said and hung up the phone. Her heart was frighteningly fast as she came out of the phone booth. Someone had written KILROY WAS HERE on the brick wall of the drugstore.

She tried to comprehend the tone of voice in which David Lannan had spoken to her, pleased, almost eager. He had been cool at first, then something had changed.

What if he thought she was coming to his house because she wanted to do it again, to strip off her clothes at his command and lie down for him? Perhaps she should do that, and then tell him. She could put up with the pain.

If he were to want to marry her, they would do it all the time. It hurt less later on, they said. You got used to it.

To take her mind off those things, to calm and strengthen herself, she thought of him as he was in school, how intelligent he was, how brave and dignified, how much he knew. Once, when Miss Turpin the Latin teacher was away, he had come to take over their class. Most teachers, in that circumstance, would have told the class to read quietly and let it go at that, but he asked what they were translating, and when he was told it was a section from Caesar's commentaries on the civil war he took the book, glanced at it, and then began to teach them about the events of the time, drawing a map on the board, freehand, and giving an outline of the history of Rome in the period. Caesar became vivid in his words.

Why, he asked them, did Caesar refer to himself in the third person? And after a few puzzled half-answers, he began to speak of how such a man was aware of himself as more than a mere cluster of selfish desires and needs and fears. He was aware of himself as an impersonal force, the embodiment of a high form of human thought and aspiration. His ambition was not for personal aggrandisement, but for the accomplishment of a human possibility, the furthering of civilization. He was a man in whom the history of the world came to a new stage, and, knowing this, he saw himself objectively as Caesar, the Roman general, the creator of history.

The next day, when Miss Turpin returned, the translation of Caesar's words began to seem important, her insistence on accuracy justified. These were the words of Caesar himself, who made history.

At the bottom of the small hill that led to David Lannan's house, Edith stopped for a moment by the streetlight. The night was quiet, and she thought she could hear a tiny humming from the bare bulb under its metal apron.

The house at the corner was huge, unlighted, and the pale yellow illumination cast by the bulb made its high gables stand out against the sky. Edith wanted to run. No, she would not be crazed and hysterical. Would not. She climbed the hill.

His cottage looked almost dark, only the slightest trace of light at one of the windows. The place across the road was brightly lit, the curtains open, and she was glad that he had left the door unlocked for her so that she would not be seen waiting.

As she crossed the porch, she was blank and vacant, not a thought in her head. She had no words. Opened the door.

Inside, the hallway was very dim. A little light came from the room ahead of her where she knew he was waiting. Everything was close and quiet, as if the house were empty, but she could feel his presence beyond that doorway.

The room she entered was lit by four candles in a high brass candelabrum, and for a long, stark moment she could make no sense of anything else. The first thing that explained itself to her eyes was white, a plaster mask of a human face, the eyes closed: a death mask. Maps on the wall, shelves of books. A framed portrait. A small oval frame surrounding a black silhouette on a white background. A huge print of a battle. Beneath it, a wide table on which tiny model soldiers manned their guns, drew up in ranks to fire, fixed bayonets, prepared their horses to charge, swords swinging in the air. The flickering candle-light made the little figures undulate like a swarm of ants.

"This is Austerlitz," his voice said. "I don't do it often. It was the perfect night for you to come."

She recognized the figure, of course, the white breeches tucked into high black boots, sword in its scabbard hanging at his side, the dark-blue coat with its high collar and gold epaulettes, the hair combed forward over the brow in Roman fashion. Even his face seemed to have taken on the slightly distant expression of the portrait that hung on the wall behind him.

She could not bear to see this, and yet the hypnotic candle-light forced her, painting the face and figure with a seductive oily glamour.

She was running down the street, her chest pushing loud rhythmic noises out of her, hard, unstoppable, painful gasps.

She could not tell if these were a wild laughter or if she was only crying her heart out.

# Chapter 9

They had done everything they could to kill him, and he was still alive, but isolated, on his own, too far forward to get back to his own lines, surrounded by German trenches and gun emplacements.

They had done everything they could to kill him. As his company came down the hill under the oak trees, the valley in front of them still silvered by a morning haze, the sunlight dim and distant, the shells began to fall. From behind them they heard the steady roar of their own artillery; they had been promised a huge and lethal barrage to prepare the way for them, but the way was not yet opened; they were met by a thousand explosions, shells falling, bursting, the scream of metal fragments, and they forced themselves on, running down the shallow hill in the haze and smoke, dropping to the earth. Ralph ran with Tart Beamish on one side of him and Eldwin Tyson on the other, and near the bottom of the slope, when they threw themselves to the ground in the face of machine-gun fire from the left, Eldwin stayed down. Just like that. He was dead.

Foot by foot, they had made their way forward into a

shallow gully where they were sheltered from the machine-gunners on the heights beside the town, and in the gully they had waited for the tanks of the North Irish Horse.

Waited.

When the tanks didn't appear, the captain worked his way back along the gully until he could get a look back toward the woods where they had started their advance. Two tanks had been immobilized as soon as they struck an unmapped minefield, and the others had retreated to the edge of the woods. From there, they were firing toward the town.

There would be no support from the tanks, and as they moved out of the gully toward the grain fields that were their next objective a mortar shell took out their signaller and his wireless. They were cut off from headquarters. At the edge of the grain field, sown with wheat now green and knee-high, was a wire barrier, and Ralph and Tart set up the bren and fired as fast as they could toward the machine-gun positions that overlooked them while two other men set grenades to blow the wire. Once into the grain field, the handful of men still alive worked their way down a slight incline to the right and went to ground, the slope providing only a little shelter from the machine-guns that tore up the earth around them. Panting and shaking, their bodies tight to the ground, they lay there and waited for the next platoon to come through the wire. No one appeared, and the German mortars were dropping shells behind and in front, bracketing them. Chunks of mud from the explosions fell on them. Soon, the mortars would have the range. Ahead of them, and to one side, were a ditch and a piece of stone ruin that would provide a little more shelter than this bare hillside.

Ralph was the first to go, and as he ran he heard a mortar shell explode behind him, as if it might have fallen on the very piece of land where he'd been lying. As he dived behind the low wall, he heard bullets from a machine-gun smashing chips off the stone all around him.

No one else came to join him there. He could hear more rifle and machine-gun fire, a scream. He didn't dare lift his head to look out, but he waited, expecting that a man's body would come leaping over the little stone wall at the end or perhaps crawling on its belly from the little ditch behind him. Nothing appeared. The world ended a few feet away where the hill of earth met the half-clouded sky.

The war had become very small. He was a single man concealed in a tiny stone ruin and surrounded by the fortifications of a strong and determined enemy. There was no point trying to go forward; one man was not going to break through the Adolf Hitler Line. It was equally impossible to go back. The Germans still controlled the ground, and he would be killed as soon as he stood up.

Ralph leaned back against the wall. Something was ringing in his ears, an explosion, the explosion behind him in the field as he broke for the shelter of this stone ruin. He had no way of knowing what had happened there behind him, but the ringing in his ears was like a message. Something blew up, clouds of mud thrown high, the thin stems of the grain flattened. He was seeing it now, even though he hadn't seen it. But he couldn't tell what had happened to the men.

How long ago was it they had started down the hill?

Was it only minutes since Ralph had seen the body of Eldwin Tyson motionless on the ground under the trees, seen the open eyes staring at him as he climbed to his feet to run toward the German positions? Empty eyes that meant death. Eldwin had been with him since they had come ashore in Sicily. Now Ralph and Tart were the only remaining members of that platoon.

Ralph heard the explosion again, examined the picture that formed in his mind, as if he might see where Tart was, what had happened to him. He tried to imagine it, that Tart was dead.

The noises of battle were farther off now, the Canadian artillery still thundering in the distance, the shells falling somewhere; perhaps where the attack was succeeding. The sound of the nearby German guns was desultory now. There was no second wave of Canadian attackers coming, not yet. It would not come until the tanks had found a way around that minefield; then they would send in reinforcements, and sooner or later they would fight their way to the place where Ralph was hidden.

Unless the Germans came for him first.

He didn't think they'd bother. Even if the machine-gunners realized he had got successfully under cover, they wouldn't risk lives to capture a single man. If he was taken prisoner, it would be by accident. The only real danger would come if the Canadians retreated, and anything more than a short tactical retreat was unlikely. Since they had come ashore, they had moved steadily forward, through summer and winter, and now into summer again.

Ralph listened to the sounds of firing and tried to make out how the battle was going. There was a lot of heavy action to the south-east on the far side of the town and beyond. Men and tanks and guns drove forward, and if they could move quickly enough they could get control of the road that ran through the valley to Rome. For a few moments Ralph wondered if he should try to find his way back, to rejoin the battle, but he knew he'd never make it, and in the circumstances a live soldier tomorrow was worth more than a dead soldier today. There was nothing to do but quietly camp out here in the middle of the German lines and wait for reinforcements. Reinforcements? It wasn't reinforcements he needed, it was rescue. Somehow the platoon had outrun the rest of the regiment and their own communications, and now Ralph had outrun the rest of the platoon. He had only two options, wave a white flag and get the Germans to take him in, or sit tight.

Sit tight.

His bladder was aching, so he eased himself over on one side and pissed down a crack in the stones, then, feeling he had taken possession of this fragment of ruin, he studied it; he had the Bren, and he tried to work out whether he should set it up on the legs ready to fire. Simpler not to, he decided, but he took a fresh clip of ammunition from his pack and filled the magazine. He laid the Bren on the right side of him, the carbine on the left, then opened his pack and took out a chunk of sour army-issue chocolate and began to bite off little chunks. In the fear and excitement of the morning before an attack he'd been unable to eat much, and now he felt very hungry, but he decided that he should make the food last. It might be a while before the Germans withdrew or the Canadian forces got this far forward.

The ruin where he lay had been a small shed or even an

animal pen of some sort, and the remains of the wall were only a couple of feet high. To keep himself concealed, he had to stay in a position that was half sitting, half lying. Probably he would be less easily visible if he took off his helmet but he was still expecting renewed shelling, a rain of shrapnel fragments. Somewhere behind his back he heard the grinding of the treads of a tank, a German Panzer, crawling forward over some stony obstacle. It was moving from left to right, coming no closer.

Past the end of his low shelter, the earth sloped downward and then rose through a field of grey twisted olive trees into a patch of woodland, and across the little valley he could see in the distance a corner of the hill where the Canadian troops had started their attack. The cloud was heavier now, but the morning haze had lifted, and the details were clear. He saw two stretcher-bearers, small bent figures, with a wounded man on the stretcher between them. They were a long way off, part of a story that someone was telling him, a story about an army and its failed attack and how the stretcher-bearers and medical orderlies were tending the wounded. The first-aid posts would be full of men groaning or crying out, and the bodies of the men who had been killed would be piled in rows ready for burial when the pressure of battle eased. As he watched the tiny figures move on that distant landscape, he had a picture of it from above, the litter of dead bodies like pop bottles and candy wrappers after a picnic. Trash. Living men who made jokes and had families somewhere, and now they were scattered across the fields like meaningless debris. He wondered if Eldwin Tyson still lay where he had fallen, the open eyes staring at the heavy grey sky.

As the months of battle went on, Ralph had more and more moments when none of it made sense. He looked up the slope to his left where there was a patch of grass with scarlet poppies growing in it and, beyond it, some woods. He could crawl up there, through the grass, into the trees, and walk until he was lost. Didn't a man have the right to run away when they were doing everything they could to kill him? Didn't he have the right to save himself?

Soldiers had no rights except to obey and then to die. And between times to drink and plunder and enter any woman who would have them. Some men were at home in that world. Tart was. He was fearless, apparently without any sense of his own mortality, and at war with the whole world, including the Canadian army. Ralph preferred to let the stupidity pass him by, to lie doggo, offer the minimum necessary obedience and be invisible. But to Tart it was all part of his personal war.

It wasn't clear why Tart hated the Italians, perhaps partly for the Catholicism he had been taught to despise, but hate them he did, refusing to see them as new allies or as a passive populace that hated the Germans after being under their power. He regarded them as defeated enemies, and he treasured every story of attacks on Allied soldiers by young Fascists, every rumour of atrocities under Mussolini. He plundered Italian houses, not for anything he wanted especially, but to enforce the message that they were a defeated people and ought to be cowed and miserable.

In battle he and Tart were perfect together. Ralph was quick to sense danger or to see opportunity, and his shooting was very accurate. Tart was inexhaustible, and battle produced in him a fierce energy that drove the two of them forward. They had become like two halves of one man, in love with their own skill, the efficiency of their killing.

The chocolate was finished, but Ralph was still hungry. No one was moving on the little patch of hillside that he had been observing. Now and then the machine-gun emplacements above him would fire a short burst. The clouds were massing as if it might soon start to rain.

Maybe it was time for the ball game. Ralph tried to ration himself, for he knew if he played it too often, it would lose its magic and be useless, and there were so few things left that gave him comfort. Once a month he wrote to Verna and Edith, but it was growing impossible to find anything to say. But the ball game brought back home and comfort.

He'd started it a few miles out of Ortona. They'd had two days of desperate, frantic fighting in the mud and cold of a ravine south of the town. The wind and rain of December were as much the enemy as the German paratroops, who held onto their positions with ferocious tenacity. Once Ralph had seen a man die when his feet slipped and he was crushed under the treads of a Sherman tank that was struggling to force its way through a morass of mud.

When they were pulled back for a few hours, Ralph had begun thinking about home. He'd needed some comfort, some escape. Among a party of Italian refugees he saw a little girl who reminded him of Edith in the photograph that he carried with him, and that had made him think of how Edith had gone to the ball games and sent him the results.

At first it was just a daydream, himself back home, the team about to play an important game, but the effect was so powerful, such a relief from the emptiness and cold and fear, that he had begun to develop the fantasy in more and more detail.

He played the game slowly, imagining every pitch, the movement of every player on the field. It always started with the field itself, the way it would look in July, the grass in the outfield bleached and dry, but still green under the trees that grew at the edge of the park. He would decide just what time of day it was, and place the sun in the sky, see the patches of shade that began to fall on the dusty earth of the diamond. Ralph would walk out into the dirt of the diamond and scuff it a little with his cleats and breathe in deeply the just slightly cooling evening air, and then he'd look at the bleachers, and carefully he'd examine the faces of the men and women and children sitting there, the biggest crowd on the rows behind the bench of the home team where they could chat back and forth with the players on the bench.

Then Ralph would put the spare bats and a pail of soft-balls in place at the end of the team bench, and the people in the seats behind the bench of the visiting team, and then he'd look off across the park at the street where now and then a car would go by or a group of children or an old couple out walking the dog, and beyond that he would sense the geography of the whole town, and only when he had all of this in place he'd glance back at the home team's bleachers and see that Verna was there, and Edith, and then he'd allow the players to take up their positions on the field, and he would carefully picture each one, and as he placed them on the field he'd have to be aware of who was at bat and whether there were any base runners, and as he did this the game would gradually take shape in his mind. Today it was the top of the seventh inning, and the home team was behind by one run. The first batter on the visiting team would be the first baseman, who batted left-handed, so as the team ran onto the field they moved into positions that favoured right field. They tossed the ball around a few times while Bob Knechtel, their pitcher, threw a couple of warm-up pitches, then they tossed the extra ball off the field and got set to play, Ralph setting himself a little wide to the left of second, and Morry Truscott playing deep and to the right of first.

Ralph went through the whole team in his mind, examining stance and position, looking for weaknesses before the first pitch was thrown.

It was a ball, outside. Cec Diebel, the catcher, threw the ball to Billy Butts at third, and they moved it around the infield and then Ralph tossed it underhand to Bob Knechtel. All the infielders kept up a bit of familiar chatter.

The pitcher threw again, his arm curving behind his back and then quickly forward with a final snap of the wrist to add spin to the pitch. Low, but good enough for a called strike. The batter looked back at the umpire and lifted his shoulders expressively. The chatter in the infield grew louder. The next pitch was outside, but the batter swung, hard, but late enough that the ball was smacked across the diamond toward Viv Nelson, the shortstop, who was playing his position a bit shallow and had to dive quickly to his right to field the ball. By the time he got his balance and threw to first, the runner had got a good start, and the ball slapped into Morry Truscott's glove just as the foot came down on the bag. The base umpire called the runner safe, and Morry argued the call but, knowing he'd never win, he soon abandoned the argument.

Carefully, pitch by pitch and play by play, Ralph played out the first half of the seventh inning. Sometimes he would stop and examine the score-card that he carried in his mind to see what one of the opposition players had done in a previous inning. By taking his time, he managed to make the half-inning last until late afternoon. Once the game got started, it took all his concentration to play it; there was so much to do, to keep everything straight for all nine men on the field. Still, he had only two and a half innings left to play, and he was a little afraid of concluding the game. He could start another, but he feared that it would never be quite the same. With this first game, he knew that as soon as he started the war would vanish, and he would be back there in the park on a summer evening, and fear and the knowledge that they were trying to kill him would retire, at least momentarily. He needed the respite. Without it, he might go crazy.

It was starting to rain. Maybe, once it got dark, he would be able to find his way back to his own lines. For now, he could only pull his steel helmet down lower on his head and hunch closer to the wall and let the rain soak him through.

Over the stink of the truck's exhaust, the night breeze brought the smell of summer vegetation, unmarked by the smells of battle: cordite, smoke, gasoline. They were outside the war zone, on leave, three days in Rome. Beside him in the back of the truck, he could hear Tart mumbling his little rhyme, like an obscene prayer.

When Ralph got back to his own lines behind Acquino, a day and a half after the original attack, he found he'd been recorded as "missing in action" along with Tart and

half their company. They'd got isolated when, after first
losing their tank support, the Edmontons, who were to
attack behind them, had been fought to a standstill, and
all the reinforcements had gone to the left flank where
Canadian troops had broken through the German lines.
But over the next few hours several more men, including
Tart, had straggled back to regimental headquarters. Tart
had survived the explosion of the mortar shell and had
gone to ground in the crater it left.

In early June, news had come of the capture of Rome by
the Americans fighting forward from the bridgehead at
Anzio, and two days after that, news of the assault on the
Normandy beaches. Suddenly there was a feeling that
this war might eventually be over, and just at that point,
they were pulled back from battle into reserve camps for
rest and training, and occasional leaves for those who'd
served longest. Now Ralph and Tart sat in the back of an
army truck that was carrying them to Rome.

Rome: he couldn't get a grip on it, somehow. It was a
name from books. As the truck bounced through the
dark, the leafy branches of trees sometimes knocking
against it where the road narrowed, Ralph tried to imagine
Rome as a real city where men and women lived, but it
wouldn't take shape. It was the home of the Roman em-
perors, the Pope. In school he had studied the ancient
Romans; he could remember pictures of them in their
togas, and the soldiers with swords and helmets and something that looked like a short skirt. He remembered an
uncle, a fanatical Orangeman, who used to go on about
the evil power of Rome; for him, Rome was the name of
everything dark and fearsome. It was strange the Protes-
tant horror of Roman Catholics. Ralph liked observing the

priests and nuns in the Italian towns; there was something comforting, proper, about the black figures passing by.

They were riding away from battle. For a year they had known nothing but fighting, with short breaks, enough to draw breath, but no more than that. He had watched men succumb to what they called "battle fatigue," the simple inability to continue to seek out death, to ignore the instinct for survival that told you to disobey orders, to hide or run. You could see on their faces a terrible edge of horror added to the usual pallor of men after battle. When an order was given, they would start to shake, and they would go forward, with empty, dead faces, for as long as possible, and finally they would crack. The new troops sometimes talked foolishly of cowardice, but when you had been here a year you knew that it was all unnatural, that all men had their limits, and some broke sooner, some later. Ralph suspected that if he didn't have Tart beside him in battle, his rage hurling them forward, he might have reached his own limit by now. He had Tart and the baseball game, and his own intuitive skill in battle, the archaic instinct that had so far never been wrong, that allowed him to fire blind and hit the mark.

What would he do in Rome? Drink and look for whores? He wished that Phyllis might be there to meet him, to take him into the blind sweetness they had shared. He wanted relief and comfort, but he didn't want to climb on top of some old prostitute who'd just serviced a platoon of GIs.

The truck slowed for a curve. They would be in Rome soon. What would that mean? For a few days, he would not have to take orders or face death, but those were the only things he knew how to do. The army had decided that he needed a rest from it all, and they were probably right. Another few weeks of fighting, and something in him would have broken. It was hard to remember anything except fighting. His dreams were dreams of battle, populated by the dead.

Eldwin Tyson: one death he couldn't forget, maybe because it was so sudden and arbitrary, because it had happened a foot away from Ralph's shoulder, to Eldwin who had been so young and simple and faithful, always writing home once a week, though the words came slow and hard. Then he lay dead, staring at the grey sky.

Ralph didn't write as often as he should. Edith was eleven years old now, and the letters she sent him were more mature, carefully constructed letters in which she searched out events from the life of the town that she thought would interest the distant man who had been her father. He wished she'd tell him a little more about herself. He couldn't imagine what she was like. When he tried, he saw her alone and lonely. Sometimes, she said, she went to Vi's and sang and played the piano. Vi was teaching her about music.

Ralph was pleased that she was learning to play the piano. She could play his old opera records, he said, whenever she wanted. But then, after he had written those words, silence fell over him like a net. Nothing more came. There was nothing in his head that he could tell her.

Maybe in Rome. He'd see the sights and write to her about them. She could tell her class in school the things he'd seen.

Eleven. What was that like? He tried to recall what he'd been like at eleven. He thought it was about that age, eleven or twelve, that he'd seen Verna Sinclair for the first time, and been struck by how pretty she was. Was some boy thinking that about Edith? No, he must be wrong; eleven was too young. He must have been older than that, mustn't he? Had it really been so long since he had seen Verna and fallen for her? Looking back like this, he felt trapped in the inevitability of it all, as if the boy who had seen a pretty girl and admired her in silence had already borne in him this future, marriage and war.

Had he joined the army to run away? Maybe. Ralph had tried not to admit to a certain disappointment in his marriage, but there was so much of him, so much of the world, that Verna preferred not to know or touch.

Maybe all this death, the emptiness inside him, was his punishment for betraying Verna, wanting to get away from her to some freer, more adventurous world. This was his freedom, the opportunity to shoot other men, to see them fall and die, to walk in terror of the hot flying metal that would scorch and tear his own body. He could have stayed at home. He was older than a lot of the men in his platoon, the only one with a wife and growing child – except one poor boy who had knocked up a girl in England and married her.

The particular horror of Eldwin Tyson's face was its youthfulness, those empty staring eyes gazing out of a smooth childish face. Ralph couldn't imagine what his own face was like, but he thought it must be lined and ancient. A man over thirty? What business did he have here? To kill and be killed, like all the others.

Once, in England, lying half asleep in Phyllis's arms, he had thought that this was what he had joined the army to find, a manly, irresponsible life, a woman who would love him even while knowing he would soon be gone; it was easy, this life, and he had felt hard and brave. Now he knew the rest of the story.

"When we get to Rome, we'll teach them who we are, won't we?"

It was Tart's voice close beside him, and yet it seemed as if it came from the night, from the grinding of the truck engine.

"Only three days," Ralph said.

"Eyetie vino is piss," Tart said, "but hell, we'll drink it anyway."

The truck hit some kind of hole in the road and all the men in it, their bones shaken, grunted or mumbled. The truck rumbled on toward Rome, which had once been the centre of the world.

It was the mixture of the height of the buildings and their closeness that gave the city its weight, the sense of power, of something monumental. The nights were hot, and the room in the *pensione* was dusty and close, but it was a real room, with a real bed where Ralph could lie alone and listen to the sounds of the night city outside the high French doors that gave onto a small courtyard where there were bicycles parked, and water ran constantly from an open tap.

The day before, he'd gone to see St Peter's, astonished by the size of it all, the way a group of nuns, their faces almost hidden under their wimples, their black gowns drifting behind them, had looked small as ants as they passed under the huge columns around the square. He had gone inside, surprised to find that he was moved by the splendour of the basilica. He observed the figures bent in prayer, a priest sitting in a confessional, reading his breviary as he waited for someone to come to confession. It was all calm, ordered, peaceful.

Back outside the church, some Italian had given him an impromptu historical lecture and demanded a few lire. Money, cigarettes, chocolate, even army rations were valid currency in the city that was quick with an undercurrent of busy life even in the circumstances of war.

The towns they had fought through were different, made victim of both armies, half-buried in rubble, grateful for liberation from the Germans but terrified of the destruction, the cold, the hunger and poverty. Afraid too of the remaining *Fascisti* who were concealed among them, still eager for revenge.

Rome was cynical in the face of war. The Germans had not destroyed the bridges; they had left it an open city, and so it was, wide open. The men walked the streets every evening in their dark suits and white shirts and ties; they maintained a face of respectability − but the soldiers who were stationed here would tell you that anyone and anything could be bought. When you looked at the Roman ruins, the Forum, the Colosseum, the huge baths, the walls of such unbelievable height, the tremendous stone vaults, you knew how the men and women who had grown up in the shadow of these things felt they had seen everything, that they were the inheritors of the fragments of a great empire, and that nothing could astonish them or shake their cool detachment in the face of their knowledge. They loved to talk for the sheer pleasure of it, but beneath the bravado, the noise, they saw it all with a cold eye.

Ralph had been filled with a kind of blank astonishment as he wandered through the city, standing among the trees on the Palatine Hill and looking across the valleys to the other hills, or wandering in a dim over-grown garden in a cloister built into the baths of Diocletian, the garden running to seed, odd pieces of ruin lying about it, or looking from the river toward the huge monument that was St Peter's. See Rome and die, they used to say, and somehow Ralph felt he understood that.

This city was the end of something.

He and Tart had separated when they arrived, then met by accident last night in a *trattoria* that was popular with Allied soldiers. Ralph had gone there for a meal of black-market army-issue bully beef dressed up with tomatoes and oil, and had spotted Tart in a corner. Tart had waved him over, poured him a glass of wine and begun to recount his adventures, how he had knocked down some Italian kid for offering to sell his sister.

"Catch me selling my sister's ass to some guy in a soldier suit."

"Might be different if you were in the middle of a war."

"Maybe," Tart said, then laughed. "Hell, she'd make a better deal selling herself. She can strike an awful bar-gain, old Doris. When I was a kid, I'd try to get her to show herself to me, you know the way kids are. Well, she'd make me pay through the nose. Candy, comic books, whatever I had for a one-second peek. She knew the price of that little piece of real estate."

He poured Ralph another glass of wine from the large flask in front of him.

"This kid said his sister was real young and pretty. Maybe I should go back and find him, after all. You should have seen the fat old woman I had last night. A nurse on her like a Holstein. Once she was on her back I had a hard time telling her from the mattress."

Ralph laughed and drank down the wine.

"I don't suppose you ever have to pay for it, eh, Ralphie?" Tart said to him. "Smart, good-looking guy like you. They just come looking for you, don't they, like that pretty one in England. What was her name?"

"Phyllis."

"The rest of us chasing tail all over the countryside, and the prettiest girl in half of England just comes up to you in the pub and introduces herself."

"I struck it lucky that time."

"They can't leave you alone."

He threw back a glass of wine and made a face.

"This vino is pure piss. Have some more."

He poured a couple more glasses.

"So any beautiful girls been chasing you around Rome?"

"No."

"There must have been a couple."

"No. I've just been seeing the sights."

"So have I! You should have seen the bush on this old Eyetie whore. She could have had a nest of mice living in there, and you'd never notice.... You think they enjoy it, these whores?"

"I don't know. I doubt it."

"I wonder, you know. If they feel a goddamn thing. I'm pumping away like mad, and she's just lying there. I wanted to give her a good smack just to wake her up. Or stick a bayonet in her ass. That'd make her jump. She made me mad, the old bitch."

The laughter was gone from his face now. Ralph

recognized the tightness of the flesh, the dangerous anger. Ralph reached for his glass, and for a moment they sat in silence. Tart looked toward him.

"You're a good guy, Ralphie," he said. "One hell of a good guy. We were lucky to hook up together."

"We keep each other alive," Ralph said.

"It's more than that," Tart said. "A hell of a lot more."

Was it? Ralph couldn't say. Probably not, for him. It was something that happened in war.

"You got to be about the best shot in the Canadian army," Tart said.

"We make a good team," Ralph said.

"Yeah," Tart said, "you smart and me crazy."

"I think we're all crazy now."

"You feel like that?"

"Sometimes."

"I don't even know what I'm doing any more. You give me a gun and I kill people. I'm good at it. I like to fight, always did. But now I don't know what I'm doing half the time. I'm in the middle of banging that old whore, and she's just lying there, making me mad, and I started to think how I could kill her. How many people have I killed already?"

"We're all a little crazy, Tart."

"Where the hell did you learn to shoot so good?"

"I don't know. It just happened."

"You go out hunting?"

"Not much."

Tart signalled the *trattoria* owner for more wine.

"Let's get drunk and find a couple of girls, Ralph. How about it?"

"Not me. I'm going to sleep for twelve hours, same as last night."

"You got some kind of rule, you don't pay for it?"

"No."

"You just know you don't have to."

Tart took another big swallow of wine. Ralph noticed that his eyes were a little unfocused.

"So tell me," he said, "what you been up to while I've been chasing whores. You been looking at these big old churches?"

"A couple of them."

"They got those little boxes in them, where you tell the priest all the things you did wrong?"

"Yeah."

"My old man told me how the priests love to get in there and get all the dirt. How you did it to her and how many times. You wouldn't get me into one of those. If you ask me, that's why the Eyeties are such lousy soldiers, telling the priest everything, how you been a bad boy."

Ralph felt as if something inside of him had gone to sleep, as if this were a dream of war, as if he and Tart were nightmares in the mind of the ancient imperial city.

He stood up to go.

"I'm on my way," he said. "I'll see you on the trip back."

"You just going to leave me here?"

"You'll be OK."

"Yeah, I'll just drink this piss and go crazy. Why not?"

Tart reached out and took hold of his arm, gripping it fiercely in his big hand.

"Fuck 'em all, eh Ralphie? Except you and me."

"Yeah." He turned to go.

Tart had picked up his glass of wine, as if in a toast.

"Fuck 'em all."

Outside, Ralph turned and walked through a maze of narrow streets toward the river to stand and watch how the lights were reflected in the broad sweep of the water. It was a big, powerful river, the Tiber.

Ralph got up from the sagging bed where he'd spent the last three nights. This was his last day in Rome; the truck would pick them up at 1800 hours, and his leave would be over. He couldn't tell if he was rested, if he was more able to fight. Certainly he'd slept as he never had before, twelve hours of unconsciousness every night, and yet he felt that the city had only deepened the emptiness that was inside him. Maybe it was a mistake to turn down the whores who pestered him, but Tart seemed no happier for whatever release he'd procured. Ralph knew he wanted too much more than a whore could offer him.

He washed in a little cabinet at the end of the hall, standing naked and splashing water over his whole body, drying himself on the thin towel the old man who ran the *pensione* had given him. The towel was soon soaked, and in the hot damp air his skin remained clammy as he put on his trousers and walked back to his little room. He dressed himself carefully, aware of being in an odd state of mind, lonely, and yet not wanting company, unable to imagine speaking to another human being.

Ralph let himself out the heavy locked door of the *pensione* and his boots clattered on the metal stairs as he walked down to the street. Outside, the life of the ancient city went on in the hot morning sunlight. Two black American soldiers walked by, laughing. Down the street a number of Italian men sat at a sidewalk café. For six more hours Ralph was free to move among these people, as if the world existed, and then he would go back to the training camp, and then back into battle, the narrow, vicious world of combat. Told to attack in the face of heavy fire, he would go, and would kill those who got in his way.

As he walked down the street, he saw an old woman in a black dress and kerchief sitting in the ruins of a building. The centre of Rome had not been heavily bombed; the worst damage was in the suburbs, but here and there the bombers had created new ruins beside the old ones. The old woman was crouched in a shady corner, breaking off pieces of bread, putting some in her mouth and handing others to someone who was hidden from his sight.

Ralph stopped at a bar and had a cup of ersatz coffee and a chunk of bread. In the corner of the bar were some old brown picture postcards, and Ralph bought one to send to Edith. It was a picture of the Colosseum, and when he came out of the bar, he turned to his right and began to walk toward the Roman ruins. He'd seen them already, but it was a place to go. Half the pleasure of being on leave was the freedom to make such arbitrary decisions.

He passed a hole in the earth, where there were fragments of walls and arches, and in the corners of the ruins he saw several wild cats, thin and spooky. Two young Italian boys stood on top of one of the walls and threw stones down at one of the cats in a narrow alleyway beneath them. Ralph wanted to shout at them to stop, but the absurdity of it all, that he, a hired killer brought from far away, would defend the half-starved cats from the half-starved children, stopped him.

Rome, this city at the end of the world, knew better.

Ralph walked past the hill of the Campidoglio, and the huge monument to some Italian king. Across the road, he saw a poster of Mussolini that had been defaced, but not taken down. Down at the end of the wide road, he could see the mass of the Colosseum. He would walk there and write the card to Edith, telling her that as he wrote he was looking at the original of the picture on the card.

When he reached the Colosseum, there was a crowd gathered. An American military ambulance was there, and a number of armed MPs were carrying something out of the ruins. A number of Italians stood near him, watching, along with an American soldier.

"What's going on?"

"Don't really know," the American said, "except one of the MPs said they found a body in there." He turned and spoke to one man nearby in fluent Italian. The man answered him.

"He says it's a girl. Somebody saw her in there, and they called the MPs."

Ralph turned away. He didn't want to know. He had come to Rome to escape from killing. Soon enough he'd be going back to that world.

He walked away from the crowd and up the hill where he sat on a bench in the sunlight and closed his eyes. He could hear the distant sounds of the city, and he tried to find words to write on the card.

# Chapter 10

She woke from a dark, oppressive dream, a landscape all in ruins that went on for miles, endless. Nothing but broken columns, huge arches, vaults and tunnels in the side of hills, and peopled by a strange small tribe of men who were holding prisoner everything good, everything loved. She had been looking for someone, though it wasn't clear who it was she sought.

Or wasn't now, awake, the dream sinking back into the lost kingdom of sleep. She lay still, the images of the dream fading, but the sense of oppression remained.

No doubt the image of ruins had its roots in her long aimless walks through the city in these last few weeks as she tried to fill the empty hours with motion, striding past one after another of the ancient Roman sites, depressed by the randomness of time's amputations, the colossal rhetorical gestures of the buildings, the stricken grandiosity.

Now the weight of those ruins, her own inability to find the strength to confront them, had invaded her dreams. In the dream she was powerless, as now, waking. The heavy drapes in her bedroom were drawn, and it was very black, though beyond the bedroom door there was a trace of light from a window that caught the illumination of a streetlamp.

As a girl, she had stood on a stage for the first time in *H.M.S. Pinafore* and had caught a glimpse of what might be hers, but with no idea how easily it might be destroyed, how deep and dark the emptiness would be when it was gone. Now her nights were full of voices from the past insisting that they had not been given half a chance. She might have told the truth to David Lannan. Or her mother. She might have raised a child. She might have married. Her life might have been crowded with family and friends.

Who was it she had lost in the dream? In her life, she had lost everyone, and as a result she had, with some care and some courage, created a person to be. Acknowledge, though, that when she had been desperate for love it had been given to her. She had tried to remain loyal to those who had given it. She had listened to Nancy Longridge only because Faith Riordan, her first teacher, had sent her, and though she had never believed that virtue would be rewarded she now found herself enjoying the lessons she gave. The girl had brought her flowers. Had brought too an eagerness to learn, a remarkable talent. And the heavy weight of that husband. He had a certain intensity, grant him that. The image of David Lannan's smooth face came into Edith's mind. How was any imaginative girl to choose between men who would bore her and men who would destroy her?

Herself, she had chosen solitude, or been chosen by it. Then had the luck to find Ezio as a friend, a protector, a surrogate for her lost father. But Ezio was growing old. As her father (now threatening to become unlost) must be. She tried to calculate his age, to see him, that vague figure of childhood memory, with forty years added.

Another life came into existence in front of her eyes, a life in which Ralph and Verna grew old together, the conventional bickering of an ageing couple half expressing, half disguising the pained entrapment.

She remembered a night in her childhood when she had wakened to the sound of shouting voices, the strained hard voices of her parents downstairs, and she had lain still and fearful, waiting for the absolute disaster that could be the only end of this. Then something smashed, a door slammed, and she heard a sequence of short awful rhythmic cries, in her mother's voice, but worse, and then the house was silent.

The child lay in bed, scared, uncomprehending, but ready to take her father's side, imagining where he might go, worried for him out there alone in the night.

Did any marriage escape such dreadful moments? Did any marriage have enough in it to make them worth surviving, worth transcending, or at least forgetting? No, she had always thought, and for years she had warmed herself with pride in her independence, but now what was she to think of her dry fate? Perhaps the arrival of her father would resolve something – if that arrival ever took place.

Would he be old, crippled, in need of care? She was no nurse, it was not in her.

Surprising to her, though, how protective she felt toward Nancy Longridge, but what she wanted was to encourage the girl's strength, her talent and intuition. She imagined the two young people in their bed in some

other part of Rome. The corrupt chastity of that man's
Christian lust.

Chastity. Oddly likeable word in ways, with its suggestion
of cleanliness. That was the only true chastity, a washing
of the mind with light, so that the body's hungry acts
went on in a bright clean place.

Would she have wished someone in bed beside her to
tell that thought to? There was not, would not be. The
men her age were married or impotent or somehow
ruined. She was alone, would be alone, though sometimes
she imagined Nancy Longridge, at the end of her planned
stay in Rome, packing off her husband and remaining.
She could move in with Edith, and Edith would teach her
and draw Ezio into the development of the girl's career.

A young man, a small, shambling man, mumbling half-
aloud, had pulled a knife from his pocket and was
slashing a brightly coloured Communist election poster
from the wall of a building near Sant' Andrea. Edith stood
a few feet back, fascinated by his wild energy, his small
bent figure a sudden focus for all the noisy activity of the
street. She speculated on whether the intensity of his
attack was political or whether it was something more
arbitrary that enraged him, the bright colours, red and
yellow and green, or the mere presence of the poster on
that wall at that moment.

Cars rushed dangerously down the Corso Vittorio
Emanuele. Men and women climbed on a bus. The man
tore at the poster, then turned and vanished in the
crowd.

Edith saw things, these days, with such a flare of
immediacy around them, as if she had just come back

from the dead. It had been like that sometimes after singing a very demanding performance. For days or weeks she would live inside the music, the sound of her voice ringing through her the only reality – and then afterward it was like a convalescence; the world came back and presented itself, and it would be as if she were walking, speaking, seeing, for the first time ever.

Every day was a little like that now. Her life was remaking itself.

Or not.

"Don't you think it's going to go out of date and disappear?"

"Opera? No."

"You make me feel how exciting it is," Nancy said, "how grand and spectacular, but it still seems…old-fashioned."

"So does your religion to a lot of people."

"But that isn't the same."

"Old stories."

"But…Christianity isn't the same thing."

"How many people in your church would want to sit and listen to three hours of the *St Matthew Passion*?"

"Not many, I guess."

"Look at all the operas that are being made into films these days. Bergman made *The Magic Flute*, Losey did *Don Giovanni*, Peter Brook's *Carmen*, Zeffirelli's *Traviata*, all sorts of others, I imagine, that I've never heard of. There's something in the great operas that people always come back to. Maybe now it's so expensive, people will have to see it on film or television, but it won't die."

Nancy was watching her intensely, a little smile on her face.

"What shall I do with my life, Edith?"

"Something wonderful."

"Like what?"

"What you have in you to do."

"What if I fail?"

"We all fail. All we can do is try to fail at the highest possible level."

Nancy laughed. Her face was beautiful when she laughed, and Edith could no longer quite remember the ordinary, unremarkable face she had worn the first day. It was gone. Rome and the challenges that Edith gave her and the way her voice and sensibility responded to those challenges had taught her a new kind of freedom. Perhaps even a new kind of happiness.

It was a cool day, but warm enough in direct sunlight that three or four people were sitting at tables outside the bar. Edith and Nancy sat inside, but near the window. Across the piazza was the church of Santa Maria in Trastevere where Lee had gone looking for some early Christian inscriptions, remains of one of the earliest Roman churches. In the middle of the square, two little boys climbed on the fountain, watched by a pair of gossiping mothers.

Edith lifted the cup of cappucino to her lips and sipped the scalding coffee that slid into her mouth from under the foam of milk.

"I'll remember that," Nancy said. "All we can do is fail at the highest possible level."

"I'm not sure it means anything," Edith said, "but it has a nice ring to it."

"Like music."

"I suppose."

Lee had come to meet Nancy at the end of her lesson.

As always, he brought a chill tainted air with him when he entered. Edith tried to give him instructions about finding the church he wanted across the river, but it was tricky, and Nancy finally suggested that Edith come along with them. Lee was unresponsive, grudging, but Nancy insisted, and Edith had led them down to the Tiber and across the little pedestrian bridge, the Ponte Sisto. Someone had left a pile of garbage burning part way across the bridge, and Lee stopped to observe it, contemptuous of such an offhand attitude to civic cleanliness.

They made their way through the narrow streets of Trastevere to the piazza containing the church, and Edith and Nancy settled down in a bar while Lee went to confront the ancient building.

Edith looked across the piazza, where four baroque stone saints gesticulated on the railing over the church porch, the same grey colour as the fountain in front of them, the church itself a miscellany of the dusty orange earth colours of this part of Rome, the mosaics on the front glowing a little in the late morning sun.

It was pleasant to sit here with Nancy, sipping cappucino, talking about the girl's future, but beyond this moment, beyond this sunlit morning, what was there for Edith herself? What was her own life to be?

The ruined city of her dreams was her own life.

"I like this," Nancy said, an echo of Edith's thoughts. "Sitting here with you, hidden away somewhere in Rome. I've never imagined that I'd be doing anything like this. Every time I write to my mother to try to tell her what it's like here for me, she writes back and tells me not to drink the water."

A good-looking Italian in a well-cut suit stood at the bar drinking his little cup of espresso. He looked at Nancy appreciatively, then tossed back his espresso and left.

Edith saw Lee's narrow figure coming toward them from the church, moving, as always, as if he were in flight from something. As he came through the door of the bar, Nancy smiled at him.

"Idolatry," he said, as he sat down at the table.

Edith lifted her cup, refused to be drawn.

"Did you find what you were looking for?" Nancy said.

"Yes, I suppose. A few inscriptions on the outside of the church. But then I went inside. I should have known better."

He looked at Edith.

"Have you seen those mosaics in the apse?" he said.

"Years ago. I hardly remember."

"They're idolatrous. Jesus and Mary — I suppose that's who they're supposed to be. Some oriental king and queen, that's what they look like. He has his arm around her, as if she was his consort."

"Is there only one appropriate image?" Edith couldn't stop herself from responding.

"I'm not sure any image is appropriate. 'God is a spirit, and they who worship him must worship him in spirit and in truth.' I think that's the beginning and the end of it."

"You were born out of your time," Edith said. "You should have been with Cromwell and his church wreckers."

"The golden calf gets remade in every century."

"And often very beautifully. Men and women like to make lovely things."

"They should be living godly lives."

"According to the divine plan as interpreted by you?"

Edith looked down at her cup, almost empty, lifted it to her lips to stop herself from saying any more. Across the table Nancy looked pale and miserable. Probably that was his intention. He had seen on her face a dangerous happiness, and he had destroyed it, had made evident his power.

Tyrant. Pious tyrant.

# Chapter 11

The city was stone and ice and a dangerous pattern of moving steel, cars and buses and streetcars. Edith stood on the street corner, unable to move. She knew that she had been standing here for a long time, and soon, if she did not move, someone would notice her and speak. If so, she would lie. She had grown skilled at lying in the last few months, and could look anyone in the eye and tell whatever untruth she needed to protect her.

She was not yet adept at lying to herself. She waited, impatiently, for that faculty to come, for it offered the only comfort in life that she could foresee.

Behind her was the hospital. She could not look back; that was one of the rules, that she could not look back. But she could stand here and feel its presence and refuse to go away. If she looked, she knew, she would run to the door and down the long bare halls that smelled of antiseptic until she reached the maternity ward, and she would demand her baby be given to her. It was all clear in her mind, the way she leaped up the steps, the fast walk down the hall, not even slowing where the floor was wet from mopping, for she knew that she would not fall, that her feet were winged, and as she passed, the sick and dying observed her with approval, for she was returning to claim her child.

Probably the child was gone. They did not tell her. She had never held the little thing, not once, only heard them tell her it was a boy, and then it vanished and she was resting and being given a cup of tea and returned to a room with green walls. They believed it was best for her to be told nothing, as if it had never happened. Even if she ran back into the hospital, her son would not be there.

A social worker had come to discuss the birth certificate with her, a pleasant woman with a slight stammer, and when she asked about the father, Edith had insisted that the birth certificate say the father was unknown. Mother: Edith Fulton, age nineteen. Father: unknown. She told the social worker she didn't know who it was.

"I don't believe that, Edith," the woman had said. "I don't think you're that kind of a girl."

Edith bit her lip, hard, so as not to cry, and insisted; she didn't know who that child's father was. Then she had rested a few days, and they had told her that she could go.

"Do you have someone to meet you?" they said, and Edith lied and said she did. Someone would have come, someone from the home for unmarried mothers where she had spent the last four months, the object of charity and pity, but she had not told them when she would be leaving. She wanted to walk away from it all, free, clean. Except that she dreamed about her baby, and she knew that the dreams would not stop, not for a long time would they stop. There was an emptiness inside her where her child had been and now was there no more. She would get used to it, somehow. No one would ever know. She had sent her mother lying letters with no return address, inventing a world with a job and friends, and in a year or so, when she had found a real world to fill her letters, she might, now and then, go home for a weekend. She had never told a soul that she was pregnant; she had no regular boy-friend to create suspicions. No one would know. No one.

Only she could not move from her place on the sidewalk outside the hospital.

Even though she knew that her son must be gone to his new parents, that he was in a strange house somewhere, held in the arms of a woman who had been unable to conceive a child or unable to bear one. Edith pictured her as a woman with a weak heart, pale and slender, beautiful in a certain kind of way, but almost transparent, needing to rest every afternoon, unable to take strenuous exercise. Her husband was well off, a lawyer or a doctor, very loving and patient with her; they would have someone come in to help her with the heavy work. But what would happen when the boy grew bigger? Would she find herself desperate if he was a little high-spirited, didn't always obey? Would she come to believe that he had bad blood, was born of some prostitute, some cheap half-crazed woman? She might give up on him, send him away to an orphanage. Edith was horrified to think it.

The huge swelling of her belly was gone. There was some puffiness, but she was almost thin. Inside her, there had been a person; she had felt it move, and now it was gone to this sickly woman who would slander the child, send it away. She must somehow get the child back. So close behind her, the hospital building; it was like a huge magnet, pulling at the atoms of her flesh, the hair flying out from her head and rising toward it. She must not turn around.

She could not stop thinking of the thin pale woman with the weak heart, who would not know what to do with the little boy as he grew strong and robust. Edith could even see the living-room of the house where the woman lived, a large room with a picture window in one of the new ranch-style houses. In front of the window was a low bench, French provincial, all the furniture was French provincial and upholstered in a dusty pink, and the woman herself wore dresses that complemented the shades of the upholstery, a dim grey colour her dress was, and she was cuddling Edith's baby to her dry breasts without realizing how she would come to hate him. It was wrong, all wrong. Edith's breasts were not dry — after the birth, they ached with fullness.

Edith had seldom spoken to the other girls at the Home; she didn't want to be one of them. It was a place to hide, this house just outside the city where half a dozen pregnant girls waddled about and wept and exchanged vulgar confidences. Edith was too proud to tell her story, to ask for their sympathy, and she had got the reputation of being stuck-up. Rightly, for she was. Stuck-up. There was one girl, a fat stupid girl named Marie, who read Archie comic books from morning to night, reading the same ones over and over, either unable to remember the story or not caring that she had read it a dozen times. Then suddenly, one day, Marie had broken out in rebellion. Over dinner she had announced that she was going to keep her baby.

"You can't do that, Marie," Mrs Ehrlich said.

"I can. I'm going to. It's my baby and I'm going to keep it."

As if roused and wakened, appetite suddenly brought to life by her own rebellion, she began to cram food into her mouth, more and more of it, swallowing it half chewed.

"Marie, stop that," Mrs Ehrlich said.

"I'm going to keep my baby."

She gobbled more food.

"You can't. It wouldn't be right. A baby has to have a father."

"I'll get one," Marie said. "I can find someone to marry me. I can find lots of guys who'd marry me."

Mrs Ehrlich looked toward her, as if taking aim.

"The boy who got you in trouble wouldn't," Mrs Ehrlich said.

Marie stopped pushing food into her mouth and sat perfectly still, a piece of spinach hanging over her lip. Then she spat out the mouthful of food onto the plate and ran from the table. There was a silence as deep and heavy as the silence of a church during prayer. Edith found herself staring at the pile of half-chewed food on Marie's plate and imagining that it was the slaughtered body of a child born before its time, and the thought was so frightening that for a moment she was convinced she was in a kind of madhouse, that the pregnancies of all these girls were imaginary, that they were only overstuffed with inadequately masticated food. Dizzy and ill, she had risen from the table.

"Edith," Mrs Ehrlich said, "you're not finishing your dinner."

"I'm sorry," Edith said, "I don't feel well."

"We mustn't let Marie upset us. She'll settle down. I'll talk to her this evening."

She did, and nothing more was heard of Marie's plan to keep her baby, but now, standing paralysed on this street corner in downtown Toronto, Edith knew that Marie had been right. She was too late, though, for Edith had signed papers, had put herself in the hands of the law, had given her son to that weak inadequate woman.

A few steps away, a man was standing still, watching her, and Edith suddenly got the feeling that her thoughts were shown on her face, that this man had observed every detail of the scene with Marie, had seen Edith waddling away from the table, had even known about the sickly woman who had stolen her baby. She started across the road, not caring which way, choosing the light that happened to be green. As she walked, she was aware of a little soreness between her legs, where they had put in stitches, and the prickly feeling where they had shaved her, and she was afraid that the man could tell these things from the way she walked.

As she hurried across the road, she could feel his eyes on her back, and she struggled to walk perfectly normally, and when she reached the far side she kept moving, not looking back until she came to the pathway to a large brick house. She waited there, as if she were considering going in, and took the opportunity to look furtively back. The man who had been watching her was gone. A group of young people, probably students, came out the door of the house, laughing together. She looked at the sign on the lawn. The Royal Conservatory of Music. As the group of students, a boy and two girls, moved past her, she stared at the sign to avoid catching the eye of any of them, but she was aware that one of the girls looked toward her, a pretty girl, with pale blue eyes and straight dark hair. As she noticed the girl's eyes glance past her, she was tempted to speak, to ask the girl her name, what she studied here, how she lived her life. There was a whole universe of lives around her, substantial, encrusted with family and friendships and ideas and ambitions, while she herself was a solitary ghost, connected to nothing. She had been attached only to the child which was a part of her, but now it was gone.

The girl was gone too. She had receded back into the invisibility of her distant mysterious life. Edith stood alone. Perhaps inside this building, that pretty girl with the striking eyes and hair, the bright, healthy skin, studied singing, learning how to let beautiful sound pour from her throat and fill the air. Edith hummed to herself a little phrase from *H.M.S. Pinafore*. Until now, she had kept it out of her mind, for safety.

> *Sad is the hour when sets the sun,*
> *Dark is the night to earth's poor daughters,*
> *When to the ark the wearied one*
> *Flies from the empty waste of waters.*

Who was the girl who had sung those words? Where was she now?

Now. This moment on a cold November day when she stood on the sidewalk staring at a sign. Until this moment, everything was *then*, was different, written in a foreign language, and similarly, all she observed around her, the men and women on the street, the young people coming out of the Conservatory, existed in a foreign language.

Now, here, was herself, something anomalous, a freak, a misfit. She must find her way back into the fabric of the world. Her existence was a dropped stitch, and she must very carefully replace it on the needles that would knit it into the fabric of life.

Edith remembered how once or twice one of her friends had spoken about coming down to the Conservatory for piano examinations. One of her friends: ordinary people came here and studied. The girl who had glanced at her had not looked very unusual, except that she was so pretty.

Edith walked up to the door and entered. From far off in the building, she could hear the muted sound of a piano playing. There was something dim and old and reassuring about the place. It reminded her a little of Vi's house. Boldly, Edith searched until she found a secretarial office, but when she found it, and the two women inside looked at her, she was frightened and mute.

"Yes," one of the women said. "Can I help you?"

"I want to take lessons, to study," Edith heard herself saying.

"What kind of lessons?"

"Singing."

"Yes, I see," the woman said. She was like the man outside, looking at Edith as if she could see her whole story written on her face, as if she could observe her shame, her separateness, how lost she was.

"Who did you want to study with?" the woman said.

The question was a trap. She couldn't answer. It was a way of proving that she didn't belong here, but she forced herself to speak, she was in the middle of it now, there was nothing for it but to be brave.

"I don't know," Edith said. "I'm not from Toronto. I just got into town."

Telling the lie was a kind of relief. As long as she had the presence of mind to lie, they couldn't trap her.

The second woman looked up from her desk. She was a younger woman with skin that was reddened and broken out, but there was something alert and thoughtful about her face.

"I think Mrs Riordan is free at this hour," she said. "Maybe she should talk to her."

"I guess that would be OK," the first woman said.

They gave Edith instructions, stairs and halls and doors, to get her to Mrs Riordan's office, and Edith was sure that she wasn't hearing any of them, but once she was back outside the secretarial office, she remembered enough to get her to a corner of an upper floor where there was a solid door, dark-stained wood, and on the outside, a small sign that said Faith Riordan. An old-fashioned name – comforting.

She knocked. There was a voice inside, and then movement, and the door opened.

Faith Riordan was a small woman, with grey hair pulled into a bun on the back of her head, a fresh complexion, a large nose and jaw, rather brown teeth showing when she spoke, and dark eyes that met Edith's directly. Her body was bent a little to one side, and she leaned on a cane. She had an accent, English but not quite.

"They sent me here. They said I could talk to you."

There was something about the words, so bare and awkward, that seemed wrong, inadequate for this woman. There was a strength about her, a dignity, that forced Edith to take possession of herself.

"I came in to ask for information," she said, starting again, "about taking singing lessons. The women in the office downstairs said that you might be free to talk to me about it."

"Come in," the woman said. It was neither friendly nor unfriendly. Edith liked this woman who wasted nothing on unnecessary politeness. She followed her into the room. In one corner stood an upright piano, with music open. Nearby, beneath a small window, was a table with straight legs and a bentwood chair pulled up in front of it. It was covered with piles of music, and a few notebooks and pens. Behind the door were shelves of music and books, and in the centre of the room was a rocking-chair with a pillow against the back, a pillow covered with a petit-point of red roses. Beside the rocker was a small table with a teapot on it.

Faith Riordan propelled herself to the rocker and sat down, leaning her cane against the wall nearby. She indicated the straight chair to Edith. Edith sat there, and the dark eyes confronted her once again. She was uneasy being looked at, but it wasn't like the man on the street, or the secretary. Edith no longer felt that her secrets were being revealed, shamefully, to strangers, yet she felt as if the woman was seeing into her.

"Tell me why you want to sing," the woman said, and Edith began, quite properly, like a grade-school student

delivering a recitation, and then, quite suddenly, she was
sobbing and telling this woman about the baby that she
had lost, and once she had started she couldn't stop,
until she was telling her things, not who the father was,
she still couldn't say that out loud, but almost everything
else, and the woman had got to her feet – even while she
was crying and babbling, Edith observed the awkward
movement with which she got up from the rocking-chair
– and then she was standing beside Edith, stroking her
hair, comforting her in a soft crooning voice.

Then it was over, like a storm that passes, and Faith
Riordan was giving her Kleenex and telling her where to
find the washroom to wash her face. When Edith came
back to the room, the woman was seated at the bench in
front of the piano.

"Now," she said, "we must hear you sing."

"I'm not sure I can, any more," Edith said.

"The voice will be a little thick," the woman said, "after
all that crying, but we can hear what we need."

She played notes and asked Edith to sing scales up and
down, trying out all of her voice from the lowest notes to
the top. Often the sound felt strained and awkward, but
Edith went on, putting herself in the hands of the woman,
who played and listened and made no comment.

"Well, Edith," she said at last, "you certainly have a
voice there. It's clear and accurate, and you have some
range and power. How badly do you want to sing?"

"It's all I have left," Edith said, and it was only after she
had said the words that she knew they were true.

Faith Riordan looked at her for a long time, and the
dark eyes were luminous and powerful.

"I must give you a chance to sing a little song," she said. "Something you did in *H.M.S. Pinafore*. Do you know what key?"

Edith tried to remember the key signature for "Sorry her lot."

"I think it was four flats," she said. "But in the minor."

"F minor, then," the woman said and struck a chord.

Edith heard the familiar sound of the chord and began to sing. Faith Riordan made no attempt to accompany her, only sat staring at the piano, then part way through the verse turned toward Edith and watched her attentively. Edith reached the end of the first verse and paused. The older woman was pushing herself up from the piano bench and limping across the room, stopping just in front of Edith, the intense brown eyes looking into her own. Edith noticed the deep wrinkles in the woman's face, the darkness of the pouches under the eyes, the deep lines running from the nose to the edges of the mouth. Faith Riordan reached out and put a hand against her cheek.

"All right, my darling," she said, "we will make you a singer."

Then she turned away and lowered herself to the rocking-chair.

"We must set a time for lessons," she said. "When are you free?"

"I don't know," Edith said. She was so happy at the woman's promise that she would be a singer, that she only half minded looking foolish. "I just got out of the hospital," she said, "and I haven't made any arrangements yet."

"When did you get out of the hospital?"

"This morning."

"And you came straight here."

"I didn't mean to, but I saw the sign and came in."

"Why didn't your family come and pick you up?"

"I didn't tell anyone."

"Oh, yes, I suppose you told me that, didn't you? But in all that crying, who was to remember details?"

"Could I phone you when I get settled?"

"Of course. Where are you going to stay?"

"I'll find a place."

The woman was shaking her head.

"You are a remarkable young woman."

'I'll find a place," Edith repeated. She felt confident now that she would, though when she walked out the hospital doors all she could think of was to sleep in some alley.

"What about money? Do you have money?"

"Yes."

"How much?"

"Fifteen dollars."

The woman reached into a corner behind her chair and pulled up a large brown purse; she searched in it for a change purse and extracted from that a folded ten-dollar bill.

"You must pay me back, I'm not rich, but I don't want you going hungry before you find a job."

"I'm sure I can find a job soon."

"But you won't get paid right away, will you?" she said.

"I'll manage," Edith said.

"Yes, I'm sure you will, but take this for now. You will pay me back, and you will have your lessons to pay for too."

"I can do it," Edith said. "I know I can."

That day, Faith Riordan had given her the address of

Willard Hall, the WCTU residence for young women which was close by and not too expensive. Edith stayed there only one night, then found herself a room in a house near Bloor and Christie. The house was not very clean, but the room was in an addition built on the back, and the landlord agreed that she would be able to sing there without disturbing the other tenants. The same day, after telling what she hoped would be her last set of complicated lies, she got a job at Eaton's, filling orders in the catalogue department. Edith had to eke out her money till the first pay-cheque, and she would have run out of food except for Faith Riordan's ten dollars, but as soon as she had money in her hand, she phoned and arranged to go for her first lesson. She tried to give the older woman the ten dollars all at once, but she insisted that Edith pay it back a little at a time, and once again she proved to be right. Having paid for the room, bought a few dishes, and paid for her first lesson, Edith was down to her last few pennies by the time her next pay-cheque came.

It was a great pleasure to Edith to receive that pay-cheque every week. She liked having money she had earned in her hand. She had taken control of her life, and she refused to remember the parts of the past that gave her pain. When they began to come back, she scrubbed the floor or sang difficult exercises until she was exhausted and the thoughts vanished in sleep.

The progress with her singing was astonishing to her, and even Faith, if unsurprised by the development, seemed pleased. Gradually the voice became easier, a friend who rewarded her with delight rather than an enemy lying in wait to trip her up. Every day when she got home from work, she spent the first hour singing scales and exercises, vocalizing on each of the vowels, one after another, changing vowels on a single note, starting exercises with different consonants. She enjoyed these exercises in pure sound, the simple pleasure of feeling her mouth and face tingling with resonance. Her teacher had sketched for her all the resonating chambers of the skull, and sometimes, as she sang, Edith could imagine them, all full of light and air.

After an hour of vocalizing, she would make herself something to eat, something cheap and nourishing that could be done on her little two-burner hotplate. And after dinner she would look at the music she had been given to learn. She wasn't a good reader, and without a piano she found it difficult, spending half her time finding notes on her pitch-pipe. After a few weeks, and at Faith Riordan's suggestion, she began singing in the choir of a nearby United Church, and she was able to arrange to go to the church some evenings and use the piano there.

She still wrote to her mother from time to time, and now she was able to write the truth, about her job, her lessons, the church, and finally, as if by accident, she included a return address. The first letter she got in reply was not from her mother but from Vi.

> *Hi kiddo,*
>
> *Verna came in last night after dinner and showed us your letter. This job sounds better than the last one, and we're all real pleased*

*about your lessons. When you're famous, we'll
brag about how we knew you when you were
three feet high and had no front teeth.*

*Mabel says you sound a lot happier than
you did for a while there. You know Mabel,
what a worrier! But I always knew you were
going to be something special, even when
Verna was having fits worrying about you.
That kid's got her head screwed on right, I
always said.*

*Glad you're singing in that church too. Some
of these ministers are dopes, but everybody
has to admit there's something to it. You just
have to keep going and not ask too many
questions.*

*Things here are just the same. You know
what it's like, but Mabel and I, we often think
about you and remember how proud we were
of you when you were in that show. I'm having some trouble with my stomach, but it won't
hurt me to lose some weight, will it?*

*Keep your chin up, kiddo.*

> *Yours sincerely,
> your friend Vi*

The letter made Edith cry, and it started to bring things
back, so she put it away and didn't look at it again, but
when she wrote to her mother, she put in a special note
for Vi and listed some of the pieces of music she was
learning; she thought Vi might find some of them familiar.
    As the winter went on, Edith began to wonder if she

should get a better job. It had become clear that if she was going to sing seriously she would need some lessons in musical theory to supplement the little she had learned in her high-school music class, and she would need more money to pay for those. So she began to search the want ads for a better-paying job; then Faith Riordan found a solution. One of the teachers at the Conservatory had two small children and was willing to trade lessons for babysitting.

During the summer, Edith was offered a job replacing one of the soloists in the choir of a church in the east end, and in the fall, with Faith Riordan's support, she got an audition for a solo position with one of the bigger churches in the centre of the city. The audition itself was harrowing, and Edith was sure that her merely adequate sight reading had lost her the position, but a couple of days later there was a note in the mail offering her the job.

The pay was quite good, but as well as learning all the choral music she had to prepare a solo for every fourth service, an evening service one week, a morning service two weeks later. It was before her initial performance at a morning service that she had her first serious attack of nerves and stood at eight in the morning staring out the window of her little room convinced that she would be unable to open her mouth, that there would be no sound but ugly croaking. She began to think that she would have to phone Bruce Updegrove, the organist, and tell him she couldn't do it, that she'd have to quit the job.

Trying to calm herself, she made a second cup of tea, couldn't drink more than a sip, set it aside and lay down on the bed, shivering with cold. Just after nine, she went down the street to a phone booth where she called Faith Riordan, at home, something she had never done before. The voice that she listened to was both sympathetic and firm. She must not back down, must not quit, or she would cause dreadful damage to her own self-confidence. All singers went through this sometimes. It was necessary to keep on with it. Once the time came to sing, it would be all right, the habits that she had learned by repeated practice would take over. Edith had always obeyed a piece of advice that Faith had given her early on: if you are a professional, you do not practise until you can get it right, you practise until you cannot get it wrong. She had made the music part of her, worked until it was in her muscles. When she needed it, the voice would be there.

For a few minutes after she hung up, Edith felt more comfortable, but then the panic started once again. She left her room early to walk to the church by a long roundabout route, in the hope that walking would calm her, and it did, a little. She found herself on empty downtown streets, where with everything closed for Sunday there was a strange ominous quiet. Then, just as she was about to turn a corner from one deserted grey street into another, a drunken man stumbled out of a narrow space between two buildings, stared toward her as if there was something shocking about her appearance and fell to the pavement in front of her.

She stopped and stood still. He lay there, only a few feet away, and she couldn't imagine what to do.

She walked close to him, afraid at first that he might be dead, but when she was right beside him, she could see his chest rising and falling with breath. He was a heavy man, bigger than she was, and there wasn't any way that she could move him. There was nothing to be done.

As she walked away, there was a continuing sense of horror at the loose ugly face that had stared at her before he had fallen, a dreadful sense of how far one could go from the human centre of the world, and the dread that gripped her brought with it a memory of the terrible morning when she had left the hospital and the night she had run down the street away from David Lannan's house. Emptiness, hopelessness, a deep blackness was so close under the surface of life. She would flag down a police car if she saw one and tell them about the man, or if she didn't see one, she would call the police from the phone at the church. They would take him off the street, put him someplace safe until he sobered up. All that was easy enough, but the look on his face, wild, inhuman, was impossible to forget.

If she didn't control herself, get on top of her nervousness, sing as well as was possible for her, she could fall into that black empty place and never get out.

It was a good life, Edith thought to herself as she sat on the grass in the sunlight. Often on a Saturday afternoon she'd come here to a park nearby and watch the children running on the grass, the men playing a pick-up game of basketball. In front of her a game had just ended. One of the players had looked at her a couple of times and smiled as if he knew her. She supposed he was being a bit fresh, but she liked his grin, and, the second time, couldn't help smiling back. It was all too beautiful not to, the way the sunlight warmed her bare arms, the speed and gracefulness of the players as they caught and threw the ball. Edith had just made arrangements to audition for the Toronto Opera Festival, which was planned for the next winter by a group who wanted to expand the productions of the Royal Conservatory Opera Association into something more professional. The world was full of possibilities. Faith Riordan sometimes suggested that Edith ought to go to Europe for a while, for further training and a different kind of experience, but there was no money for that, and right now she was happy with things as they were. She leaned her head forward on her arms and closed her eyes, letting the warmth of the sun pour over her. She had even found the courage to risk a couple of trips home recently. Little had changed. Her mother and Sid sat in the kitchen playing euchre or cribbage; Vi and Mabel dropped in to visit. Vi had lost weight and didn't look well, but she'd recently started with a new doctor and expected great things. Edith avoided the streets near the school and David Lannan's house, and she had never seen him nor heard his name mentioned. The week after she returned to Toronto, she got a clipping from the local paper, sent to her by her mother. It noted that Edith had been visiting and gave an outline of her singing career, with a prediction that she would soon be heard on CBC's "Singing Stars of Tomorrow."

"How about a Coke?"

He was standing just down the hill from her, the same grin on his face as she had seen when he was on the basketball court.

"I don't even know you."

"Sure you do. You just watched me play basketball."

"I wasn't really watching."

"Should have been. I got twenty points."

"You sound pleased with yourself."

"Why not?"

She couldn't help smiling at him.

"C'mon," he said. "I'll buy you a Coke."

Edith looked across the park and saw two lovers walking hand in hand on the vivid green grass, and remembered how often she had seen people together in couples and felt lost and lonely, afraid that these easy things of life were not for her.

"OK," she said, and stood up.

"What's your name?" he said.

"Edith."

"I'm Carl."

And that was how it started.

For a while Edith kept expecting a trap to be sprung, the secret disaster to occur, but it didn't happen. Carl was a happy straightforward man and he liked her. He had no particular interest in music, but he didn't expect her to learn all the rules of basketball or baseball or hockey. He didn't like going to church, but he'd wait for her down the street every Sunday, and they'd go for a long walk or take the ferry to Centre Island or Hanlan's Point. They'd go swimming or just lie on the grass under the willow trees, and Carl would hold her and kiss her, and one Sunday evening she did as he wanted and went back with him to his basement apartment.

It was a pleasant surprise. He was too easy a man to frighten her, and, expecting pain and shock, she discovered only a lingering sweetness that left her wanting to stay with him, to spend the night in his arms.

It was summer and her body was full of gaiety. She

took in breath and sang, she ate and made love; she was happy and shameless. There was a desperate fear of pregnancy, but Carl promised that he would take no chances and always used a safe; he said that they were effective. Once, late at night, he murmured that even if she got pregnant they'd only have to get married, but Edith refused to respond to the remark. She didn't know quite why, only knew it was something she didn't want to hear.

Toward the end of the summer, Carl once told her that they used so many French safes that he had to go to three different stores to buy them to avoid embarrassing himself, and for a moment Edith didn't know whether to laugh or not, but he seemed only amused at his own embarrassment, and she joined his laughter.

They were in the bedroom of his basement flat. The flat remained cool during the hottest weather of the summer, but there was always a certain dampness in the air, and as she lay on the bed, Edith could see a pattern of heating pipes crossing the ceiling above them. Carl liked the place because it was private and cheap; he was an electrician just out of his apprenticeship, and he was determined to get enough money ahead to start in business for himself as an electrical contractor. Though he gave the impression that he was interested in nothing but sports and love-making, Edith sensed that there was a streak of solid common sense in him. He would do well.

His apartment had nothing in it but the furniture placed there by the landlord, clothes on hangers over a heating pipe, and baseball uniform, bats, balls, hockey sticks and skates in a corner. He played basketball, baseball, hockey in the winter. His sports trophies were at his parents' home in a town a few miles north of Toronto.

Carl lay on his back on the crude bed, a box spring and mattress set on two-by-fours. Edith's head lay on his chest, and he was running his fingers through her hair and over her scalp. He had strong, simple hands, always warm even when her own were cool.

Edith wondered sometimes if all this physical joy would alter, perhaps improve her voice. Probably that was a foolish idea, but she couldn't help speculating; they were related in her mind, loving and singing. She would have liked to ask Faith Riordan, but as much as the woman knew about her, Edith was still too shy to bring it up.

Sometimes, even as she was pressed against the warmth of Carl's body, she would remember her baby, and David Lannan, and she would go suddenly cold, and Carl would seem a stranger who was invading her, and she would have to wait and lie and pretend until she could fight down the memories and find him again, know who he was, hold him as he deserved to be held.

Did she love Carl? The question was a terrible puzzle to her. He was not the sort of man she could ever have imagined for herself, so blunt and easygoing, at ease in the material world and asking for nothing more. Edith had always thought that she must have someone special, someone like David Lannan who stood out from the crowd, who was exceptional, gifted. Well, Carl was a gifted athlete, or at least a very good one, but he seemed never to have had an idea or a desire for anything more than a modicum of worldly success. He would never fail, but he would never aim high. He appeared to regard her singing as a harmless hobby, and she was even guilty of concealing from him just how hard she worked at it, the hours she put in practising and studying.

But she delighted in his hard smooth body. She'd been surprised that his skin was remarkably smooth, silken; the muscles beneath the skin were shapely and moved with such grace. When she was close to him, she wanted only to touch him. Was this love? She had no answer, only a terrible suspicion that this might be one of the many situations in life where you learned the truth only when it was too late to put it to use.

She came here, again and again, down the hall past the furnace room, into the bare (even ugly if she was to let herself know the whole truth about them) rooms where the two of them laughed and touched, but she could not imagine how this episode was to fit into the story of her life. She was learning Massenet's *Manon*, Micaela in *Carmen*, and hoping to appear in the chorus or even *comprimario* roles in next winter's opera festival; one part of her lived in that high, tragic world, while another part of her was perfectly happy to slip surreptitiously into the back door of Carl's apartment and laugh at his jokes about the number of contraceptives they used. How to make sense of it all?

It was a clear September evening when she got home from work and found a letter from her mother. Vi was in hospital, it said, not expected to recover, and she had expressed a desire to see Edith. Could she come?

Edith wandered around her room with the letter in her hand, looking at the way the sunlight caught the leaves of the Manitoba maple that grew in the yard beyond her window. The evening light was golden, and the leaves hung perfectly still. Beyond the tree was the brick wall of a factory that made small metal products for steamfitters. It was empty now, of course, the men gone home for the night. She imagined them, each having dinner with his family, and not one of them knowing, or ever to know, that Vi was in hospital, that Edith stood here with the letter in her hand staring at the way the setting sun fell on the leaves, the thick grass, the factory walls. The world went on being the world, even though Vi was dying and had called for Edith to come.

She made arrangements to get Sunday off from her church job, and on Friday after work she walked to the bus terminal and bought a ticket home. Riding on the bus, once it was out in the country, Edith became aware of the time of year as she never was in Toronto. There was a fringe of red on the edge of some of the trees, the stubble of the grain was stiff and pale. Just before it dropped over the horizon, the sun was a deep red ball, and then as the darkness gathered a harvest moon appeared, huge and orange, like a pale echo of that setting sun. Gradually the moon rose in the sky, becoming smaller and paler. Half-way, the bus made a stop at a small restaurant and depot so the passengers could eat something and use the washroom. Edith wasn't very hungry, but she ordered a bowl of tomato soup, and the thin acidy soup made a clean pleasant sting in her mouth and throat.

When she reached her destination, she called her mother from the terminal to tell her that she was home, and then walked, carrying her small suitcase, to the hospital, but when she got there she discovered that visiting hours were over for the evening. She asked about Vi, in the grip of a superstitious belief that if she did not see her immediately some disaster would occur during the night and she would be too late. But they assured her that Vi, though sedated now, would be able to see her in the morning.

Edith set out to walk home through the streets that were familiar to her from childhood, the setting where her earliest memories played out their tender sentimental comedy. As she walked, she felt constantly under observation, as if behind every window men and women had gathered to see what she had become. Whenever she saw a figure coming toward her along the street in the half-lit spaces under the high old elms, she speculated on who it might be, tried to prepare herself to nod or smile or speak, whatever might be appropriate, and she was astonished that the only people she passed were complete strangers. Of course now she was the stranger; she had been gone nearly three years.

The door of the house was locked, and she stood on the porch and knocked. Perhaps if she was a stranger here, the place would have lost its power over her.

"Edith," her mother was exclaiming, "don't you have your key?"

"I'm not sure where it is. I think I lost it."

"Did you walk all the way over?"

"I went to the hospital first, but they said I couldn't see her tonight."

"She's in a bad way. Terrible. I hate to see it."

"Is she going to die?"

"They say she doesn't have long."

"Does she know?"

"Yes. She's a Tartar, that Vi. Kept at poor Dr McAllister and wouldn't give him any peace until he told her everything."

"Yes," Edith said, "she's a Tartar."

"Are you hungry?"

"I had a bowl of soup when the bus stopped."

"How about a sandwich, I've got some ham."

"OK."

She put down her case and followed her mother to the kitchen. Every sight and sound of the house was familiar, and yet Edith couldn't get her bearings. She felt as if she might have been one come back from the dead, no longer able to quite understand the things that were most intimate in the previous life. Her mother asked about her job, about the bus trip up. She was doing her best, but she couldn't bring herself to ask about Edith's musical life. As always, she made her way around it as if it were something a little shameful. Edith realized that although her mother had sent her that little article from the local paper it must have been Vi who gave them the information.

Edith ate the sandwich, made conversation for a few more minutes and then went up to her room. She closed the door, turned on the light and stood perfectly still. Like the rest of the house, like the town itself, the room was familiar and foreign. There was the old quilt on the bed, blue squares with lighter blue ruffles, made for her by Grandma Sinclair and given to her on her twelfth birthday. The three china dogs on the chest of drawers, a Dalmatian, a Scottie and a black spaniel. For a while, her mother had given her a china dog every year for

Christmas, and Edith had dutifully found a place for them in her room, though she had never much liked them. Beside them was a photograph of her father, smiling and holding Edith, who was not quite two years old.

This was the room where she had often sat with the little silver heart clutched tight in her hand remembering how her father's figure had vanished around a corner. She would press the little heart in her hand and pray that he would be safe, would come back from the war, and when the news came that he was missing in action, this was where she had lain, crying, begging some unknown power to change it all, to make it a mistake.

Yet now that she was in the room, those memories seemed less real than when she was away from it; the reality of the bed, the dresser, the dogs, the pictures on the walls, all these present facts seemed to overwhelm the past.

She sat in the blue chair in the corner of the room and thought of Carl, tried to imagine bringing him here. It was a hard thought to encompass, Carl naked and roused, Edith laughing and shameless, in this room where she had been a little girl.

In the morning the sun was bright, and even with the blind down the room was brilliantly lit, every corner of it glowing, shining. Her room in Toronto was never like this; it was too much surrounded by other buildings, by trees that grew close by. Edith raised the blind and looked down the street where the light fell in dappled patterns on the roofs and lawns.

After breakfast, she went out into the vivid, hectic light to walk to the hospital. To reach it she had to pass quite close to the school, and she was afraid that she would see

David Lannan, though it was unlikely he would go there on Saturday. Near the hospital, she was momentarily convinced that she saw him a block ahead of her. The figure turned out of sight. She had no words for what she felt for him now, only knew that it would be unbearable to confront him, that he had, still, some power over her, some power to do her harm.

At the hospital, she tried to prepare herself for what she would encounter, but the sight of Vi in the bed was still a shock. Vi's staring eyes met hers.

"Hi, kid," she said. "You're looking great. Big city must suit you."

The words, the smile, were familiar, but there was something empty, something absent-minded about them. Vi's concentraiton was somewhere else, locked in a struggle with pain, or reaching out to encounter her death. Edith struggled for words.

"I'm sorry," she said, "that I didn't get here before. I didn't know…"

She couldn't finish the sentence.

"You didn't know how bad it was, eh kiddo? Guess I didn't for a while either."

The round fleshy face was turned toward her, the eyes too large, too intense. The flesh hung loose on the bones.

"Come and sit down," Vi said, indicating a chair by the bed. "Tell me about your music."

Edith sat in the chair and began to talk. She tried to think of everything she'd sung, any moment of interest, described her lessons with Faith Riordan, what she was planning to sing for the Opera Festival audition. Vi's body lay in the bed, her eyes closed, her big hand with its dark yellow fingernails, on top of the cover, twitching a little.

Though she thought Vi might have fallen asleep, she went on attempting to make her career sound important, for she knew that was what Vi wanted from her, and somehow, as she spoke, her life in Toronto took on more substance and she was able for a moment to feel that she had achieved something, that she was creating something worthwhile. For Vi's ears, she was shaping her life into the story of how Edith was sailing out into the ocean of the big world. Then finally she had no more words and was silent.

Vi opened her eyes and turned toward her.

"I was just thinking," she said, "how you used to sit on the piano bench with me and sing 'The Bluebells of Scotland' while I played along. And here you are, going to be in the opera." She reached out her hand and Edith took it. Then Vi rather hastily pulled her own away.

"Now don't make me start to blubber," she said. "I've got something to say to you, and I want to get it said. I talked it over with Mabel, and it's fine with her. You see I've got a bit of money in my name and Mabel's got some in hers, that came from our grandfather; and we've got the house and Mabel's got her job and a pension coming to her in a few years. So she's all set. So I talked to Mabel and then I talked to old Mr Gilder, he's our lawyer and always has been, and what I've put it in my will is that you're to have the bit of money that's in my name."

"Oh, Vi…"

"Now you just be quiet, Edith, and listen. You're something special, you always were, but you'll need to travel somewhere to study, to the States or Italy where they've got the best teachers. So now you'll have a few dollars to help. I'll like to go knowing that the money will be put to a good use."

Edith tried to say something, but she was crying and couldn't speak.

"Now you come and give your old Vi a hug," Vi said, "and then get out and come back this afternoon if you want to."

Edith went to the bed and hugged the woman. The big body was smaller now, almost fragile. Vi reached up, pulled Edith's face to her and gave her a wet heavy kiss, then held her hot face against Edith's.

"I don't want to die, kiddo," she whispered in Edith's ear. "I'm scared." She kissed Edith again. It was thick, wet, sad. "You were alway special, you know," Vi was saying, "always special."

Edith could think of nothing to reply so she just hugged Vi until she felt the sobbing stop.

"I better rest now," Vi said. "Maybe they'll give me a shot."

"I'll come back this afternoon," Edith said.

Outside the hospital, she began to walk as fast as she could, and she kept walking until the movement began to calm her. Back at the house, she had lunch with her mother and said that she'd be going back to the hospital in the afternoon. But she told her mother nothing about the money that Vi was leaving her. She would tell no one. When she went back to the hospital to visit Vi, neither one of them mentioned it.

Carl offered to attend Vi's funeral with Edith, but she turned him down. She didn't want explanations, introductions. He accepted her decision calmly enough, but surprised her by inviting her to visit his parents some weekend when she could get off from her church job again. As it happened, one of the other soloists got sick not long after and Edith had to fill in at a couple of services, so she didn't mind asking for a Sunday morning off. She'd be back in the city in time for the evening service. Edith couldn't help speculating about Carl's reasons for arranging the trip. Did it foreshadow some change in things; was it a way of making her aware that he was serious about her? At times she thought it was merely something to do during a weekend when he had no game to play. Hockey hadn't started yet, and he complained sometimes of having nothing to do. Now and then he dropped in at her room in the evenings and demanded that she go for a long walk with him, and it was hard to make him understand that she had work to do, music to study. It was just as well, she thought, that she'd never spent the money on a telephone so that he couldn't just call when he wanted company.

Carl had borrowed a car for the trip, a big 1948 Mercury, and there was a pleasant sense of adventure on that Friday evening as the powerful machine ate up the miles of highway. The trees were already bare, and the land was beginning to look dim and dormant. In the sky, dramatic streaks of cloud were lit by the setting sun, and then it was gone and a blue darkness was drawn up over the sky from the eastern horizon. Edith felt solitary, excited, too quick to notice how a tiny stream glowed dark silver at the edge of a culvert, the way dead grasses were pressed to one side. She felt as if she was breathing too deeply, and she was relieved when Carl made a joke about sneaking into her bed in the middle of the night.

"You wouldn't, would you?" she said.

"No," he said. "I don't suppose so."

When they drove up to the house, Edith was surprised at the size of it. She knew that Carl's father ran a successful five-and-dime store, and that his parents were a little annoyed that he had gone off to Toronto to apprentice as an electrician instead of going into the business, but she hadn't really thought that the owner of a large variety store in a good-sized town would be an obviously successful man.

It was a three-storey clapboard house, painted white with dark green trim, and the large lawn was well kept – recently mowed and raked clean of fallen leaves. Carl's parents met them at the door. His father had straight grey hair, neatly brushed into place. He looked like Carl but was slighter of build. The mother was a little taller than Edith, with a very bright, clear complexion and hard grey eyes. She was nicely dressed – made Edith feel as if her own clothes were shabby – and very polite and friendly.

Inevitably, Edith supposed, she was being sized up as a possible daughter-in-law, and she didn't quite now how to communicate the fact that she wasn't sure she cared to audition for that role.

Carl and his father launched into the conventional discussion of the car, the road, the traffic, the route they had taken, and his mother guided Edith upstairs to her room, a beautifully decorated guest bedroom on the second floor, with white glass-curtains, a delicate pattern of yellow flowers in the wallpaper, yellow and white towels and washcloth laid over a small table, a white flocked bedspread and two matching brass lamps with pale green shades on the two sides of the bed. The woman told Edith where the bathroom was and left her, and Edith stood in the perfectly appointed room feeling like an impostor. She did not belong here in the middle of all this perfection. She tried to place Carl in this house, but when she did he became a stranger. Who was the man with the bare cheap basement apartment who was always naked and erect and laughing? Was this really his family? Was this quiet, finely decorated house the place where he was raised? It made no sense. Perhaps he had brought her here to show her what was expected of her, that she was to be transformed, as if by fairies, into the likeness of his mother.

Downstairs, sitting at the round dining-room table for a late meal, Edith became convinced of the truth of her fears. There was nothing unkind or thoughtless about the way she was treated, but she felt as if she were at school; the teachers were patient, perhaps even loving, but inexorable. They would make her what she must be. At moments, eating the good food, feeling the calm of the house, she felt that she needed only to acknowledge the rightness of what they offered her, and she would be happy and secure.

After dinner, Edith helped with the dishes. She knew it was expected.

"Carl says you lost your father," his mother said.

"Yes. In the war."

"It must have been hard for you, growing up."

"I missed him," Edith said. She didn't want this woman discussing her father. If she had known him, she probably would not have liked him. His enthusiasm, his passionate curiosity about everything. But perhaps he wasn't like that at all. It was a long time ago. She had been forced to create him out of a few memories, a few photographs, a bit of friendly gossip. He was a stranger, and he was gone.

When the dishes were done, Carl took her out for a walk, to show her the place. Outside, his hands eagerly hugging her to him, he seemed more familiar, more like the man she knew, except that now she felt that man might be an impostor. One of them surely was. Edith was aware she must say something about his parents, said that they were very nice to her; it was the best she could do, and it seemed sufficient. When they came to a quiet bridge over the river that flowed through the centre of the town, Carl wanted to go down into the darkness at the edge of the bridge and make love, but Edith refused. It was the first time she had ever refused to make love with him, and, like everything else that was part of the trip, it seemed ominous.

Later, alone in bed in the perfectly decorated guest-room, Edith found herself wishing that Carl would come to her, but she knew he wouldn't. She wondered about Carl's parents in bed together in a room nearby. Were they hot and eager for each other? Surely not. But how did one reach that state of temperate poise from the way that she and Carl were in his apartment, hungry and insistent? Edith found it hard to believe that the woman with the cold grey eyes had ever been like that; many women weren't, it seemed, and Edith felt like some kind of freak, something cheap and common.

Carl had brought her here to show her what she must

become. She was filled with horror at what he must think of her. She had been easy and cheap. Like a whore. Well, and if she had, he could not turn her into his lady-mother by wishing it. Edith was lost and hurt, and she had no defences against such humiliations, but one day, she swore, she would achieve fame, and she would be safe. She would be…something, something extraordinary and untouchable. Proud and angry, she turned to sleep.

Saturday went by without incident. Edith had enough experience of dealing with the world from a position of cool control that when she needed the ability it was easy enough to bring back. She smiled and lied and made things go on easily enough. They visited the places in town that were of significance to Carl, drove to a farmer's market a few miles away and helped with the shopping, helped Carl's father rake the back lawn. When Carl wanted to touch her, Edith kept him at a distance.

At the end of the day, lying in the dark in the strange bed, Edith counted up the hours until they would leave and congratulated herself on surviving. Once they were gone, she knew, Carl would tell her, in one way or another, that he was unhappy about the distance that she had put between them, and she prepared her answer, aware that she must phrase her explanation in such a way as to imply no criticism of his parents. She performed the scene in her mind until she was satisfied that she could handle it.

Sunday morning they went to the large United Church on the main street of town. The choir was less impressive than Edith expected of a church that size, but she found it a relief to be standing and singing the hymns. For a few moments, her body relaxed.

It wasn't until they were standing in the sunlight outside the church after the service that Edith realized that Carl was angry about something.

"What's the matter?" she said.

He turned away from her. His father pulled the car up to the curb in front of them. Carl held the door for his mother.

"Why don't we walk?" Edith said. "It's such a nice day."

"Yes," Carl said, "we'll walk."

"See you back at the house," his mother said.

Edith waited on the sidewalk as the car pulled away, then Carl came and joined her and they set off along the street. There was a cold wind blowing toward them.

"Well," Edith said, "what's the matter?"

"Everybody in church was staring at you." His voice was tight with anger.

"What do you mean?"

"You didn't have to sing like that."

"Like what?"

"Louder than everybody else in the church."

Edith stopped walking, unable to take a step forward. She had seen one or two heads turn toward her in church; it didn't surprise her that people wanted to know who it was they could hear singing in a strong trained voice. She had even been prepared to take the attention as a compliment, but now she felt as if Carl had stripped off all her clothes and left her standing naked in the street.

"That's the way I sing," she said.

"You could have toned it down a little."

"I did."

He snorted.

"You bellowed just as loud as you could so everybody would notice you."

She started to walk away.

"I'll take the bus back to the city," she said.

He came after her.

"We don't need to fight about it," he said.

"No, we don't." She wanted him to go away, to leave her alone with her pain, her dreadful nakedness. She was shivering with cold.

"Let's go back and have dinner. We can leave right after that."

They were walking fast in the wrong direction, away from the house.

"Maybe I shouldn't have said anything," he said, "but you made me feel like a damn fool."

"I'm sorry I embarrassed you. You can be sure I won't do it again."

"People around here just don't sing like that."

"Then I have no business with people around here. I won't come again."

She felt suddenly hopeless, empty. She hadn't, for the moment, even the strength to sustain her anger. At that moment, she had nothing left to her. Nothing.

She stopped walking. Forced herself to speak.

"Let's go back for dinner," she said. "There's no use upsetting your parents."

As they turned back, Carl took her arm, and when she let him, he looked relieved, as if he thought that she was ready to forget the whole thing. Let him think that. She knew it was over between them. He had turned her to stone, and he would find her stone.

As they walked back to the house, it became clear to her that once she had the money from Vi's estate she must go away somewhere. She must make a new world where there was room for music.

# Chapter 12

Able. Baker. Charlie. Dog. Well, not any more. Able and Baker more or less, with the remnants of Charlie and Dog added on to make two companies, and those still under strength. Able. Baker. So long Charlie. So long Dog. Death. Meant you couldn't remember who used to fill the place that was filled by somebody else. Able bodies. Disabled bodies. Able Baker bodies. No Charlie bodies. No Dog bodies. But they were all just bodies. Labourers. Beasts of burden loaded with metal and explosives, pieces of guns, ammunition. Pile on the last few pounds until it's all you can do to walk. Then they shoot at you. They try to blow you up. Able. Baker. Charlie. Dog.

At least in this mud, you could dig. Unlimber your trenching tool and push the brown gum aside to make a hole for the machine-gun or the Bren. Or just dig a hole and fall in and pull the mud back over top. They were going to kill you anyway, so why not give them a hand? Save trouble for the new faces, the anonymous rein-forcements who wouldn't have to dig your grave. Dive into it. Bury yourself, the way you did every time there was an explosion, a burst of gunfire.

Ralph had been here too long. There was nothing left of him. Rest and training no longer brought back warmth or life. He was dead now, even though the bullet hadn't struck. It was there somewhere, the German bullet or mortar shell or artillery shell that was waiting for him. Somewhere behind the German lines was an infantry soldier loaded down and stumbling forward, and he was carrying the shell or grenade that would finish the job.

He shivered all the time, and sweated. He was always thirsty, but once they went up front, they had to conserve water. One of the ways they were trying to destroy him.

Able. Baker. Charlie. Death. Once there were four companies, and men sent out letters before they went into battle. The men died, and in a hundred houses wives and parents read the letters from the dead. After a while men stopped writing letters before they began to fight; sometimes they stopped writing letters at all. There was no longer anybody to write to. All you knew was what you could see and touch, and here in the rain and dark you could see nothing and touch only the cold metal of the gun. They were perfect soldiers now. Unafraid of death because they knew they were dead already, only waiting for the bullet with the right name. Unfrightened because they had lost all feeling. Except he shivered all the time, and when the noise of explosions, artillery firing from both sides, mortars, tanks, rifles, grenades, invaded his head, he would scream, as if he had to hear his own voice or he would bury his face in the mud and never come out.

He had been Mentioned in Despatches. They tried to make him a sergeant, but he refused. When he joined up, that was part of his plan, to do well and achieve promotion. Now he knew better. Not even the money could tempt him. Sergeants had to think. Thinking was deadly. It made a path into your head for the noise and the fear. And the rain. If you started to think, the rain and cold got in worse than ever.

> *Dear Ralph,*
>
> *Well, things here are much the same. People say that we're winning the war now, but who knows? I hope things are OK with you. OK here. We keep busy down at the store. Mr Franklin wants me to decorate for Xmas again this year, says I did such a good job last year.*
>
> *Edith does well in her schoolwork, but I don't know about that girl. There's something about her. I just don't know.*
>
> *Your mother is sending you a parcel, and I took over some socks I knitted. I think they'll fit OK. Your dad tried them on and said they were right for him.*
>
> *I guess it will be strange for you when you get back home after all the places you've seen. Edith liked your card from Rome. She took it everywhere with her. I guess she's getting to the difficult age.*
>
> *It's been a long time since you left, and you don't seem to write much. Your mum says you don't want to worry us.*
>
> *Not much news here. Things just the same.*
>
> > *Your wife,*
> > *Verna*

A flare went up and burst in the air above them, and the landscape was suddenly illuminated by its bright mysterious light. Ralph looked across the canal toward the German lines as the flare slowly descended on its parachute. In front of them, the narrow drainage canal shone as it slid toward the Adriatic. Drops of rain pitted the surface. In the front of their hole in the mud, the grass stems were flattened, and some of them held drops of water. On the far side of the canal was the earth bank behind which the German soldiers were dug in, and behind the bank, to the right, a ruined house from which machine-gun fire raked over them.

The flare began to go out. Ralph turned his head and looked back in the last dim light. He saw only ruins and darkening fields. Since the last mortar and artillery attack, they had no way of knowing if the rest of the company was still there. Their last orders were to stand to until first light, but it was possible that no one would come to relieve them, that there was no one left alive to do it.

Able. Baker. Charlie. Death. Four companies became two companies became one company became a few perfect soldiers, silent and untouchable. He knew that Tart was there, two feet away from him, but they no longer spoke much. They had nothing to say. They were perfect soldiers.

He heard the sound of Tart's canteen opening, and he could smell the raw warm smell of rough Italian brandy that he had picked up somewhere. He'd managed to move forward with his canteen filled with brandy instead of water. The sergeant hadn't checked.

"Want some?" he mumbled.

"No."

Once he might have worried that Tart, drunk, might doze off at the wrong moment, might get them killed, but now he had no worries. No worries at all. Just a shivering that never quite stopped. A hole where mind and memory used to be. A weariness all though him. Able Company. Disabled Company. If he put his mind to it, there might be something that he could remember. He could remember his name. He was a man named Ralph. He had a wife named Verna. They had done what men and women do, and they had made a child named Edith.

Ralph opened his own canteen and allowed himself a sip of water, but the sip made his thirst almost worse than it had been. He took a mouthful, but then he was dry again. He wanted to creep down the dike to the canal and bury his head in the water. He would catch something, jaundice or dysentery, and they would ship him out. It was a good plan, and at first he couldn't understand why he didn't do it, but then he remembered that if he climbed out of his hole in the ground someone would shoot at him.

Of course, sooner or later they would shoot at him anyway. It was only right. They had come here to be killed, to be heroes. That's what heroes did, got killed and then they weren't heroes. They weren't anything. Right now Ralph felt that he wasn't anything either way.

The night measured itself out slowly in a drizzle of rain. He tried to remember what he had seen in the field behind them during the last seconds of the flare's light. It seemed to him that he had seen bodies lying in the long grass where there had been no bodies before, but he couldn't be sure.

He was climbing up an endless slippery mud bank,

and there was no top. He buried his face in the mud and couldn't breathe.

He opened his eyes. He wasn't sure whether he had been asleep or not. He must have been asleep, but how could you have a dream so quickly? It was as if the dream was lying in wait for you, ready to pounce the second you closed your eyes. A terrible dream of endless climbing.

He heard the gurgling of brandy as Tart poured it down his throat. Ralph thought maybe he should ask for a mouthful to warm him. When he thought about it, he could taste the brandy in his mouth, and the taste made him sick. He could feel the brandy sliding down his throat, and his stomach knotted and rolled, and he thought he might throw up. He breathed slowly and deeply, and the nausea began to go away.

Somewhere to the left of them, there was a sudden burst of machine-gun fire, and he listened for an answering burst to know if it might be the beginning of an attack, but there was silence again. Sooner or later, an attack would come, but not yet. Not yet. The German soldier who was carrying his death hadn't arrived.

He wondered if he'd know when that death was close, whether all his senses would become more alert, whether he would go out looking for the death that was assigned to him, as surely as a rank and serial number and platoon and company and regiment were assigned to him.

Then Ralph knew he was hearing something, some sound, momentary, over the soft whispering of the rain and the singing of the water in the canal. He lifted the rifle and fired into the darkness, toward a sound he wasn't even sure that he could hear, and suddenly the

fire was returned, and Tart was setting off short bursts
from the Bren. A cry of pain down by the canal. A figure
in the dark, close to them, and Ralph squeezed the
trigger and saw it fall.

Ralph slid across to the Bren and held a new magazine
ready, as Tart raked the gun across the darkness, the
tracer bullets writing their message on the night. The
Bren stopped firing, and there was a large silence. Ralph
listened for movement; in front of him, he could hear a
man writhing and moaning.

"Trying to sneak by us," Tart said.

"Maybe they thought there was no one here."

"Fuckers."

Maybe they thought there was no one here. Maybe
there was no one here. The bullet with his name on it
had already arrived, and he was dead but couldn't tell.

They both sat forward, listening for any sounds,
watching for anything to move in the darkness, but there
was only the light rain. The moaning had stopped.
Probably they were safe now until morning. The Germans wouldn't try the same tactic twice.

Ralph was startled to realize that, weary as he was, his
instinct for battle was still acute, that he had heard or
sensed the men who were approaching them in the
darkness.

Perhaps that instinct would be the last thing to survive
in him.

His eyes tried to reach farther into the darkness.
Nothing moved.

No sound but the whispering rain. Ralph reached into
one of his pockets and pulled out a piece of hard tack.
Nibbled a corner off. It was tasteless, and his mouth

revolted against it. No matter how long he chewed it, he couldn't seem to swallow. He choked down the small bite in his mouth and put the rest of the biscuit away in his pocket.

The German he shot had been across the canal and coming toward their position. He must have come down the far dike and waded across.

They waited. Nothing came. Ralph settled back down, his back against the mud wall of their hole.

Able. Baker. Charlie. Death. His eyes wanted to close again. Every time he repeated that fragment of alphabet, something inside him took over, something that made him want to sleep, to turn his back on this war. He could hear Tart opening his canteen again, and he could smell the brandy. Perhaps soon it would be light, and they would be sent relief, though relief only meant they could retire a few yards and wait under mortar and artillery attack until they were told to go forward again, to cross the canal and capture some new objective.

There were rumours that the Canadians would be sent back to England, or to the battlefields in France, or even to Burma.

No one would know anything until it happened. Although they gossiped about it, no one cared. The perfect soldier had no room in his life for suppositions. The perfect soldier was already dead.

Ralph thought maybe he'd try the baseball game. The first game had ended in September near Monticello, and he was having difficulty getting the second game to work out. He kept finding that he was repeating plays from the earlier game, and as he watched one part of the field the other parts would go blank, or after a play he would look to the small row of wooden bleachers and find that they were empty, as if the spectators had all gone home, as if only the two ghostly teams were there, and even they might easily vanish. Often he'd think of playing half an inning, but postpone it until he knew he could get it right.

It was a Saturday afternoon game that he was playing this time, and the sunlight was bright and direct on the diamond. He tried to start it, setting in place all the trees, a few cars parked just off the road near the diamond. It was all veiled and shadowy, and he gave it up.

Tart was drinking down more brandy from his canteen. It would soon be gone. Ralph felt the cold coming up from the earth into his body, and wondered again if he should ask for a mouthful of the brandy to warm him, but he knew he'd never get it down. How long would this go on, being unable to swallow anything?

"Fuck 'em all," Tart mumbled quietly to himself. It was the creed of the perfect soldier. Able. Baker. Charlie. Death. Fuck 'em all. The long and the short and the tall. What happened to men who had been educated in that creed if they ever went home again? He didn't have to worry about going home. There was a piece of steel, perhaps a grenade fragment, a chunk of artillery shell, that was waiting for him. Somewhere, a long way off were people who wrote him letters. They didn't know that he was already dead.

No. He was just pretending to be dead to try and stop the shivering and he knew that if they weren't relieved before the next firefight his nerve might crack. That was why he had to go on pretending to be dead. Dead men don't shiver all the time. Dead men don't run away.

They should have a rule that after you'd killed so many

Germans you were allowed to quit. After a dozen or two dozen or a hundred. But he couldn't remember how many he'd killed. He couldn't even remember the names of the latest reinforcements or the new lieutenant. He could remember that his own name was Ralph, his wife's Verna, his daughter's Edith. He thought he could remember that, but there was something phoney about it, a trick somewhere.

Tart was walking, quietly, drunkenly, to himself, but Ralph couldn't seem to understand the words.

> *Dear Daddy,*
>
> *Thanks for the postcard from Rome. I took it to school with me and showed it to everybody. Mr Wilson helped me look up the Colosseum in the encyclopaedia. He says the Romans used to go to games there, like us going to the baseball game. But bigger. And they were cruel and killed people.*
>
> *He asked me if I'd like to go to games like that. I bet you know what I said.*
>
> *Sometimes I play your records. I'm going to save a special one to play after you get home.*
>
> *Next week is a school concert. I'm singing in the choir. We're singing three Christmas songs, but I won't write all the names. They're too long.*
>
> *Lou McPartland is running to be mayor. Grandpa says he's too stupid for anything else.*
>
> *I was saving two jokes for you, from the paper, but I lost them at school.*

*Everybody misses you. I bought some War
Savings Stamps.*

*Love,*
*Edith*

Ralph thought maybe he could see a little trace of light
in the sky to the east of them. Tart was still talking, the
words coming out slowly and intensely, addressed to the
sky or the earth or the Bren gun beside him. Ralph could
hardly hear them, but then they got louder.

"You didn't know that, did you?"

"Didn't know what?"

"No. You'd never figure it out. I knew that you'd never
figure it out unless I told you."

"Told me what?"

"I killed her."

"Who?"

"That's what we're here for, isn't it?"

"I don't know what we're here for. Not any more."

"Kill. That's what we're here for."

"Or get killed."

"Yeah. Get killed. That's pretty good too. Bang. Nothing.
Fuck 'em all."

He was silent for a second. Ralph stared at the sky,
trying to see if it was morning, if it was almost time for
them to be relieved.

"You didn't know, did you?" Tart said.

"Know what? I didn't know what?"

"I don't have to tell you about it. Fuck 'em all."

Ralph couldn't answer. The rain had almost stopped,
and there was a moment of silence and then artillery

began to fire from behind the German lines, but a couple of miles west.

"Why don't you say something?" Tart said. "You fucking deaf and dumb?"

"I don't know what you're talking about."

"You do. You know."

Ralph was watching the sky. He was sure that the east was lighter now, and there was something in the air, some tiny sound or some quality to the silence, that made him feel that an attack was imminent. And slowly, from inside him, like a voice in a dream calling him by name, came the knowledge that the bullet, or grenade or mortar shell, had arrived, the one intended for him.

Nothing to do. Nothing to be done.

Tart was mumbling again like some kind of madman telling an incoherent story that made sense only in his own crazed brain. Ralph tried to remind himself that this was his buddy, that this man had saved his life, shared food and drink and danger too with him, but memory carried no conviction.

"They won't get me down on my knees," Tart said.

"Who?"

"Any of them. They won't get me down on my knees in front of some priest. I seen them going in behind the curtain. I know what they're waiting for."

"You're not making sense," Ralph said, angrily. He was furious at the nonsense that Tart was mumbling, and at what lay behind it, something he didn't want to know.

"They're going to kill us," Tart said. "Don't you know that?"

"Of course I know it. We're all on our own out here. There's no one back there to relieve us."

"Dead men. A platoon of dead men. Fuck 'em all."

For a while Ralph felt the shivering had been almost under control, but now it was worse, his whole body shaking as if the bones were trying to dance their way out of the flesh. This was no way to die. To lose everything else first, the bottle emptied out and then shattered. Cooped up in a tiny gun emplacement with a madman. Ralph tried to think of something human and decent. He tried to think of Edith in the picture that he carried in his paybook, tried to feel her serious eyes on him. If he could imagine she was watching he wouldn't be so alone.

"She was young, you know. Just a kid."

"Who?" Ralph was almost shouting, frantic.

"The Eyetie girl in Rome!"

"What girl?"

"You won't listen, will you. Fuck 'em all. Fuck 'em all."

Ralph made his voice flat and normal.

"Tell me," he said.

Tart was silent now. He put the canteen to his lips again.

"I don't know why. I can't remember why I killed her. But I did."

"A girl in Rome."

"That's what I said."

"The body they found at the Colosseum?"

"One of those places."

Ralph had walked away and refused to watch as they brought out her body. It was just one more dead body. There was nothing he could do to help.

"Her brother was pimping for her. That made me mad. Pimping for his sister. And she pretended to cry, so I'd give her more money. She was just putting on an act, crossing herself and bawling."

Ralph had his finger on the trigger of his rifle, and the

barrel was pointed toward the voice that was telling him these things. He took the first pressure on the trigger. He could do it, so easily, and no one would ever know. One more dead body. The girl at the Colosseum, a Canadian soldier here. Blood justice. It meant nothing. One more casualty. The pictures started to come back, a rookie private with his whole stomach torn open, a jumble of organs visible inside. The leg of a German soldier lying in a ditch, covered with flies, and no sign of the rest of the body, as if the legless German might have hopped off to safety. A stretcher-bearer with blood pouring out of a wound in his neck, forming a puddle on the rock on which he lay.

Ralph moved the barrel of his rifle off to the left and slid his finger off the trigger.

There was a moment's silence. Tart had stopped mumbling. Ralph felt himself pulling away, against the mud walls of their little trench. The man might reach out and touch him. It was horrible. Empty as he was, prepared for death, he didn't want to be soiled by that touch. When he thought about the girl in Rome, how Tart had killed her, it was his daughter's face he saw, and once more his finger played with the trigger of the carbine. He could feel the way the rifle would jump in his hands as the bullet penetrated the man's body a few inches away.

"Got nothing to say, Ralphie?" The voice was bare and flat now.

"No. Nothing to say."

"She was just some little Eyetie bitch, wasn't she?"

"Somebody's daughter."

"They sent her out to sell. Her brother was pimping for her."

"I got nothing to say. Nothing."

It was light enough now, that he could see the figure of the other man, just across from him.

"If I get killed," Tart said, "you can tell them. Fuck 'em all, eh?"

Ralph said nothing. An artillery barrage had started behind the German lines, with an answering thunder of guns from their own.

A shell burst close to them and Ralph buried his face in the mud. The earth shook as another shell burst, then another. Mud was falling on his back, burying him, and as he lifted his face to breathe, he could make out the shape of Tart's body sprawled against the earth, on his back, his hand clutched over a wound in his side. Ralph crawled to the Bren and began to fire, wildly, pointlessly, insanely, into the smoke in front of them, as if it was his final duty to use up all their ammunition. He was shouting aloud as he fired, and then the earth lifted again, and he felt his face being torn open, blood, and he seized a handful of wet mud and slathered it over the wound. Beside him Tart was moaning, and machine-gun fire chopped into the earth in front of him, and then Ralph felt his own body heaving in great spastic jerks, and he was on his feet and running. They would never get him back.

# Chapter 13

"It's very cynical, isn't it?" Nancy said. She had been singing Despina's aria "*In uomini, in soldati*" from *Così Fan Tutte*.

"It would be without the music. I suppose Da Ponte's libretto is a kind of dirty joke about unfaithful women, but Mozart turns it into something else. Da Ponte shows us that women shouldn't make great high pious claims about the truth of their feelings. Despina keeps trying to tell them they're only human. But listen to the love duets. The whole opera is about duets, and the love duets after they're unfaithful are just as beautiful as the love duets with the original lover. And the vocal pairings are more natural. The mezzo falls for the baritone, the soprano for the tenor. The music tells us that infidelity isn't necessarily cheap. Love is love, and it's all wonderful."

"I don't like Despina."

"You sing her very prettily. Something in you must like her."

"But what she says is so cynical. That they should love for fun and vanity."

"She's a chambermaid. She gets to change the dirty

bedsheets. You can't talk to her about high-flown moral ideas. She's seen the dirty sheets. She knows what it's all about."

The look on Nancy's face was almost amused, as if she was a little shocked but not altogether displeased to be. She made Edith laugh.

"I thought it was only girls of my generation who thought they should save themselves for one man," Edith said. "I thought now all young women started taking birth-control pills at thirteen and slept with any-one they fancied."

"Some of them do, I guess."

"Not you."

"I didn't come from that kind of family."

"So there are still proper respectable girls out there, are there?"

"Of course."

"Who marry a man and sit at home to raise his children."

"There's nothing wrong with that."

"For those who have nothing better to do."

"Do you mean me, Edith?"

"You're not asking for my opinion, you're fishing for compliments. You know you have an exceptional voice. You know you have a talent for performance. It's your business what you do with it."

"Sometimes I don't know what to do. I want someone to tell me."

"People who give advice usually do it as a way of justifying their own choices."

Edith said the words out loud by way of warning to herself. There were too many ghosts in the room listening to her words, sitting in judgment. There were things she wished to say but could not. Not yet. The silence extended itself painfully, and Edith was relieved to hear the buzzer from the apartment door. She went down the stairs to answer.

When Edith opened the door, Lee Longridge was facing her. His eyes were bright, and they stared at her, not skittering away as they had on his previous visit.

"Is she here?" he said.

"Yes. Nancy's upstairs."

"I have to see her."

Edith held the door for him, but she couldn't bring herself to invite him in. She didn't want him inside her apartment, but she led him up the stairs, having no choice. Together, Edith and the young man walked into the room where Nancy stood, her body slack, her face blank as she waited in some kind of apprehension for her husband's words. The air was thin. Lee walked toward his wife, and Edith was momentarily afraid that he might commit some act of violence. The eyes of the girl awaiting him were large, ready for tears. When he came to her, he reached for her hand, and holding it, he sat down in the chair beside her.

"It's not working," he said.

The young woman was stroking his hair.

"Give it a chance, Lee. Give it more time."

"No. It's gone. It's gone away."

Edith watched the two of them, embarrassed, uneasy, wanting to escape the intimacy of their words, their looks.

Nancy looked at her, the expression on her face one Edith had difficulty reading, defiance perhaps.

"Lee's afraid he's losing his faith," she said.

Edith thought she might laugh aloud. She had expected …what? Impotence, adultery, anything but this.

Lee was looking toward her, still grasping his wife's hand, holding it so tight Edith thought it must be causing her pain. He began to speak. To Edith. For some reason he was determined to tell her his story. He knew she did not wish to hear it. He wished to force it on her.

"I came here, to Rome, because it was the centre of the early Church. The apostles travelled to Rome, Peter and Paul, and I believed in my heart that I could get close to their presence. That I could touch the stone their hands had touched. That the warmth of their living presence would enter me. I wanted to be a part of those early days when the Christians were only a little gathering of souls, when Jesus was a friend they could still remember, when his life on earth was still close. The Book of Acts has always been one of my favourite books of the Bible. I loved to read about them, those men and women. Who knew Jesus as a friend. A few souls building the church. The martyrs giving their lives. They found money for me to come, a scholarship, because I explained it, what I felt in my heart, how I could make the dumb facts of archaeology into a living voice. Lee Longridge had an authentic vision, I told them. I believed it. I really believed that I had a special grace. To do this work. The words would come to me, the ideas, the metaphors. It stirred my soul. When we arrived, I was so full of the joy of God. Here I was, Lee Longridge, at the heart of the early Church. I went from one Christian site to another. I could ignore the tourists. We came in winter to avoid them, but there were always some. I prayed for the power to ignore them, and I could. I was here to touch the stones the apostles touched. Then one day, while Nancy was here with you, I went down into one of the catacombs. There was something down there, the damp or mould – that was what I thought at first – that made my head ache terribly. I'd never had such a head-ache. As I went down further, it got worse. Then I said to myself it might be a sign. I truly thought that I might have a vision, like one of the saints, and I walked through those tunnels thinking I should run away from the guide, to be alone and wait. I was sure there was something looking for me down there, but the pain only got worse. It was so wet and cold. I was in the city of the dead, and my head was shattering with pain. We came to a room where they have early Christian inscriptions under glass. The names of Peter and Paul, as if the people who wrote those things might actually have known them. Words carved in the rock by hands that had touched the apostles. I thought to myself that this was what I'd come for, that this was as close as I'd ever come. I stared and stared at those inscriptions. My head was still hurting, but not so badly now. I looked so hard at those inscrip-tions, looking for a secret, looking for Jesus, my special vision, what I'd come for, and what I saw was nothing. Lines. Scratches. I was afraid it was all a fraud. How could I ever know if they were authentic? There was no way to know. And even if they were? Everything was pointless. Silly. I was just a fool. At first I thought it was a reaction to the pain, but it's gone on. Once it starts, it just gets worse. None of it means anything now. I don't kow why I'm here. We have to leave. I have to go back and find the roots of my faith in our normal life. I've realized that what I wanted was false and destructive. I was trying to escape the need for faith in some kind of immediate contact. I was wrong. I was all wrong. We have to go back. We have to live lives of faith within a Christian community. Lives of humble faith. All we're given is the Word. We have to go back to that."

The speech had come out with a snapping, percussive rapidity. Now he was silent, and his eyes turned toward Nancy, who was looking down at him as he crouched in the chair. Her face had a flat, complacent smile.

"We'd better leave now," she said.

Edith nodded. She didn't want to see any more of the naked intimacy between these two. She didn't believe his story. It was a fantasy he had created to give him power over Nancy, to drag her away from the future her voice promised her, to take her back where he could keep her under his control. Let them go. She wanted them gone.

When they had disappeared down the stairs, the apartment was very empty. And cold. Edith had made some fish soup and planned to give Nancy lunch after the lesson. She could smell the soup as it simmered on the stove. She would eat alone, after all. She was used to it.

The cold rain dropped steadily on the cobbles of the little street outside her window. She looked across the cubist pattern of roofs where old and new buildings were jumbled together; the tiles were slick with water and the sky cold. She had always loved the architectural chaos of these streets. Nothing had ever been torn down, everything patched and reused, built over or under, adapted, re-created. Around the corner was a tiny seventeenth-century church front with no church behind it; it was wedged into a corner between some apartments. The theatre of Pompey, where Caesar was killed, had stood a hundred feet from here. The building no longer existed, but the walls of the current building still had its curve, a fragment of the Roman theatre was there, buried.

It was like a metaphor for the human mind: thousands of years of history and an active hungry present all joined together in a chaotic and chance fashion.

Even in school, she supposed, she had seen history as a kind of theatre. David Lannan had made it large, dramatic, and Edith could never resist the theatrical, the grand. Faith Riordan had aimed her at German *Lieder*, but somehow Edith always veered off toward the pageantry and splendour of opera. She'd lacked the confidence for *Lieder*, the stillness. To declare herself in public, she needed all the aids of disguise and glorious setting.

Edith looked away from the cold rainy roofs and went to her piano. The score of *The Marriage of Figaro* lay to one side, and the score of *Rosenkavalier* stood open. Why had no one ever asked her to sing the Marschallin? Was she not beautiful enough? Not intelligent enough? Not German enough? She looked at the page in front of her.

*Leicht will ich's machen dir und mir.*
*Leicht muss man sein,*
*mit leichtem Herz und leichten Händen*
*halten und nehmen, halten und lassen…*

How wonderful to sing those lines to the beautiful boy you know you must lose. It must be done lightly, the Marschallin sings. To hold and keep, or to hold and let go, must be done with a light heart and a light hand.

They took place under the *anciens régimes*, those great

comedies, the world of Europe before the revolutions, the world of things as they are. Tragedy and melodrama, with their solitude and doomed loves, were the inner landscape of adolescence, with its entrapment, its longing for cataclysmic change. Comedy accepted the delights of an imperfect world. The world of middle age that she now inhabited, where the suffering solitary adolescent became tolerant of her old selves and the masked world and wished only to conduct herself with some grace. And yet the unchangeable world was crowded with discoveries, disguises and revelations. Perhaps, simply, one tired of loneliness. The Countess in *Figaro* forgave her husband, though she could not have great hopes for the Count's future fidelity. Children and parents discovered their true identities, the right lovers were paired, the music spoke of delight and forgiveness, but this was still the *ancien régime*.

In the adolescent youthful world of tragedy, concealment brought disaster, Rigoletto opened the bag and found the body of his daughter. In comedy the revelation when the masks were taken off created the possibility of love. *Contessa, perdono*, sang the Count, with a terrible poignance in the rising sixth and then the even fuller feeling of the following rising seventh as the Count repeated the word *perdono*, begging forgiveness of his long-suffering wife.

Ezio sat in the corner of the room opposite her, a tiny figure with a finely shaped face, a goatee that made it look longer, thinner, his eyes bright. They sat there, the night outside dark, a winter rain falling on the ancient city, the wild cats gone down into the tunnels of the Roman ruins. Candles burned on the black piano, their light mobile, warm. Outside, her ghosts cried out on the wind, and yet she was not unhappy. They sat, in silence, like souls on shipboard, the boat surrounded by a storm at sea, driven through darkness to some unknown destination, the star space that exists off the edge of the world. Or as if they were waiting for the beginning of a ceremony, waiting for the others to arrive, for the priest in his cloak of furs and bones to come among them and begin to chant and dance. She thought of the dead. She was not unhappy. If Ezio asked her now, she thought, she would sing for him.

"Are you well, Edith?"

"Well enough."

"What is happening with your wonderful student?"

"She's going back to Canada. To have babies. To be a perfect wife."

Ezio sipped his Scotch, studied her.

"Have you considered a trip to Canada?"

"Sometimes."

There was a pause and Edith listened to the rain against the windows. It was saying something she couldn't quite hear.

"You could be paid for a trip to Canada."

"How?"

"There is an engagement."

"No."

"You should consider it."

"No."

"It is *Rosenkavalier*. To sing the Marschallin."

"No," she said. "No. No. No."

She was still shaking a little. On the way back from the bank she had been crossing the Corso Vittorio Emanuele at a spot where it curved past a high building, and, half distracted, had walked into the road and nearly been killed by a car that seemed to come out of nowhere (a car sat in Nowhere aimed at her). Scrambling back, she had tripped on the curb and fallen painfully. A man she recognized as the owner of a small hotel nearby ran to help her up and lectured her on crossing the road with more care: everyone knew how terrible the traffic was in Rome now, it was the Communists of course, everything had gone downhill.

Embarrassed, humiliated, shaken, Edith pulled herself together to get away from him and went into a bar nearby to drink a bitter espresso while she gathered her wits. Death, imminent and personal, had been inches away. The universal visitation, addressed to her.

And so? Would the world be worse off without her? She had become invisible in these last months, a lost solitary being. Each day thousands were born, thousands died. She would make a single digit among those thousands.

Nancy and her husband were gone. The girl had made a place for herself in Edith's life, and then vanished when the man summoned her away. Left behind an emptiness without a name. Emptiness had once, when she was a singer, been a space within which the voice could expand and resonate. Now it was only emptiness.

The most silent part of the night had passed. There was always an occasional noise from the streets of the city, but now the noises were more frequent, a Vespa buzzing like the wasp it was named for, voices, distant traffic. The three of them sat where they had sat for hours, like three pieces of statuary in the Museo Barracco just around the corner from them, where Edith sometimes went to watch the shapes of life change from the geometric stiffness of the archaic material to the flowing naturalism of the classical period and back to the hieratic stiffness of the early Christian works. As the night went on, she seemed to have gone through stages like that, a whole history, had been stiff and rigid, eyes staring, untouchable, then suddenly only human, bending with the winds of feeling, and then again hard and upright.

What was she now? Tired, spent, drained of all her energy, a ruin and yet with a little flickering lamp of something burning in the draughty corridors. She looked across the room at Ezio, and saw that his eyes were beginning to close. He opened them suddenly, pulling himself awake, but then they began to drift down again, and softly, his head dropped forward.

It has been a long night. She had known when Ezio invited her over that he was plotting something, but that was no surprise. He was always plotting something for her good. He still believed that he could convince her to do *Rosenkavalier* in Ottawa.

They were settled in their chairs, drinking Scotch, when Ezio rose and walked with his careful step to the record-player, and took out a record and put it on. Above his turntable was a window, and he stood looking out, his back to her, the small neat body held very upright, as always, and Edith assumed that he was turned away because he was annoyed with her.

The music started, the voice, and Edith herself was suddenly terribly irritable. There was a kind of cloud behind her eyes as if she might be about to get a splitting headache, and she was very angry with Ezio for putting on this record, though she wasn't sure why. Something had gone wrong with her thinking, almost the way it had before she walked on the stage in Bergamo, when she could no longer hear the orchestra or the other voices. She could feel fury growing in her, and confusion along with it, and she knew that in a moment she would go and take the record and smash it. She couldn't bear the drooping passion of the tune, the way the two male voices caressed it. Tawdry, all this cheap emotion was tawdry, but at the very moment she was thinking this, her face was wet with tears, and she stood, to go to the turntable, to seize the record and break it, but halfway across the room she stopped, as if she could no longer remember who she was and why she would have this terrible destructive desire. And the tears ended, but still it was as if she had lost herself, been seized and taken over by some other presence which could blur the edges of her personality like a child's damp finger rubbing over the line of a pencil. It was a muddle, and she was bound in it; it was sticky and caressing and it stopped her mouth and eyes and ears, though she could still hear the moaning lyricism of the tune, and she knew that it was the expression of some dreadful sorrow, and still it was sugary and horrid. Once again she went toward it, to destroy it, but once again she was stopped. Someone had come into the room with them, and his voice was speaking her name, but it was a voice she didn't know, or if perhaps she knew it, she rejected the knowing. It was part of the dreadful thing that was in her brain, and Edith wondered for a moment if her brain was diseased, if some tumour or infection had invaded it. The voice was speaking her name again, and she stared toward Ezio as he looked out the window into the night, as if it might be his voice speaking to her, though she knew it wasn't.

The music ended, and Ezio turned back to shut off the machine. Click. Click.

"Edith…"

She would not turn to the man. He had designs on her. He was going to take out her brain and do terrible things to it. She would not let him.

"Edith…"

He had come close, and he was standing in front of her, trying to put something in her hand. Edith knew that she must not take the object that this man was offering her. She must not look at his face, and she must not allow her fingers to be soiled with this terrible thing that he wanted to force on her. She shut her eyes, and was aware that he had put it in her hand, and she heard that he was going away, but now she would not open her eyes. Ezio was speaking to her, urging her to look, and there was something in his voice, something protective and soft, that seemed to her condescending. She would not be at the mercy of anyone. She was too proud for that. She would look.

In the snapshot she saw a woman and a girl. It was a long time ago, and the clothes were so out of date they looked almost exotic. The girl was standing beside her mother, but not touching, and they were both staring seriously into the camera. The photograph was wrinkled and stained as if it had been carried for years.

Edith turned to the man who had put this snapshot in her hands, this old photograph of Edith and her mother in the backyard of their house. There was a huge scar down one side of his face.

He didn't speak, only looked at her, and she searched the damaged face and searched her memory for a face that had been lost for such a long time, and could find nothing. Only another photograph, that she had carried with her, and that face she could summon up, to search out a resemblance. There was. Or was not.

Her mind was clear now. The clouds around the brain had lifted, and she walked to the record-player and took the disc and broke it in pieces, and knew now that she was doing this on her mother's behalf. She was aware that this was insane, that this was acting as if she had loved the woman, and she never had, but still she would demand revenge for her mother's pain. And for her own. She sat down in a chair, and the anger found words.

They had been deceived. She and her mother had lived out their sorrow for a man who was alive. She stared at him, the pale blue eyes that she thought now might almost be familiar, and she called him a liar, a monster. Every day of sorrow, every day of loss seemed to have been transmuted into fury at the abandonment they had suffered. She could see Ezio's eyes on her, startled, wanting to interfere, but she wouldn't let him. Her wild eyes kept him silent, at a distance. He was good to her; he was kind to her, but there was a limit beyond which she would not allow him.

How could he appear now and claim kin, after all these lost years? How could he think she would accept him? Now. Where had he been? How had he dared? What excuse could he offer? What possible excuse? None. None at all. Why had he done this to them? There could be no excuse. How could he? How could he? And why?

The photograph that he had put in her hands had

fallen to the floor and lay there face down on the fine oriental carpet. The woman and child were invisible, poor souls, alone in that bare yard in the barren past. And unseen, turned to the carpet, the faces were changing as Edith stood above them, a mere observer at the poignant alterations of their lives. She had stopped shouting her anger now, but it still burned in her.

It had to do with her mother, that he had left Edith responsible for her unhappiness, that Edith had borne the weight of that dim uneasiness, that dreadful mild misery as her mother wandered lost in life, husbandless, unplaced and confused. Edith's anger was more for that woman than for herself, but he would not understand that, and Ezio would not. They would think it was mere self-pity that was causing her to cry out. She must be silent.

Her eyes moved toward the photograph on the floor, and she knew that he was looking there too, and she could not help seeing his face, how old he was, how his bones seemed thin, and she could not stop staring at the scar that covered the right cheek and temple. The mark of a wound.

How did you get the scar? she would ask him, and he would begin the story of his war and what had happened after it.

The story entered her mind with a startling vividness, as if, she thought, a space in the brain had been left for it, as if certain parts of her imagination had kept themselves free, untouched, to be ready for these events. Ridiculous, of course, to think that; it must only be the shock of it all that made her alert and receptive.

She saw it all, the man running away and hiding in ditches, in barns, stealing food, his mind, his memory shattered into fragments that wouldn't cohere. Walking for miles, knowing only that he wanted to reach the mountains, driven by terrible images of murder. He came to believe that he had killed a child, and that he must hide in the hills to avoid capture and condemnation, some animal instinct telling him to wash the wound and bandage it with rags from his shirt.

Day and night. A hundred days and nights. Half starved, half frozen, he found the ruin of a church or castle, and beneath it a kind of crypt where he was sheltered from the rain and wind, the sudden snowfalls. He was torn between a guilty need to die for his sins, whatever they might be, and a powerful cunning animal impulse to survive. He had forgotten who he was, though he was haunted by images of destruction. He had thrown away his paybook, his identification discs, and kept only a small photograph, and he would become convinced that the girl in the photograph was the one he had killed, and then he would put the snapshot under a stone in his little cave, but each time something led him to retrieve it.

There was a village nearby where he stole food, but there was little to be found, mostly scraps thrown out to the chickens and pigs.

In the last heavy rains of the winter, he became sick and feverish, too weak to go out for food, draining the last of a container of rancid olive oil that he had found in a heap of rubbish and then starving as the fever shook him. He huddled in the bed of rags and branches and waited for death.

Then somehow his dreams and delusions became centred on a little nun in Sicily, who had smiled at him, given him coffee, blessed him. He had to find the little nun and thank her before it was too late, to tell her about the child he had killed and receive her blessing.

The local priest, a certain Don Benedetto, found him, more dead than alive, unconscious, in front of the altar of the church, his wound only half healed, still raw, his clothes in rags, his hair and beard uncut for months. With Don Benedetto was a small boy who served as his acolyte. The astonished priest stared at the grotesque figure, crossed himself, mumbled a prayer, and then ordered the terrified boy to run for help.

Within five minutes the whole village would come running, brought by the news of the miracle, that the wounded body of Jesus had been found lying at the altar of their obviously blessed church.

Listening, caught up in the story, Edith knew things that the man himself had never seen. The women throwing themselves on their knees to pray. The men lifting the frail body to carry it to the priest's house, Margherita, the priest's housekeeper, a taciturn widow, stripping the body of its rags and making a thin soup to pour in the mouth, the villagers able to talk of nothing else for weeks but this visitation, taking sides, as Ralph learned later, on the issue of whether this was *Christo* himself or some potent diabolical figure who would cast the *malocchio* over them all.

Telling the story tired the old man, and sometimes his voice would drift away into silence.

"But you," he said more than once when he had stopped for breath, "I want to know all about you."

"Yes, but first finish your story."

So he would return to his tale which went forward into the years that he stayed in the village, and back into the memories of war that slowly returned to him and taught him who he was. For months he had not spoken a word, knowing little Italian, and having nothing to say, as if he had taken a vow of silence, a vow from which on some future day he might be released. His silence increased the awe his arrival had created in the men and women of the village, and buttressed the impression already held of his sanctity. Sometimes children would come to the priest's house and try to peek in the windows to catch a glimpse of the miraculous visitor. Gradually, as he became stronger, he began to do a few jobs around Don Benedetto's house, and while slowly his memories were coming to have some coherence he was also aware that in his silent listening he was growing to understand Italian, and increasingly to have a place in the life of the village. If men and women saw him, most would cross themselves, a few would spit as a defence against the *malocchio*, but these responses became more automatic. He came to be accepted as part of their lives, the silent stranger who, more and more, took on the heavy tasks around Don Benedetto's house, for both the priest and his housekeeper were well past their first youth. He cut wood, tended the priest's little vineyard and garden, and as first months, then years, went past he even began to speak, a little, in the colloquial Italian that he'd heard around him.

By that time, his mind was clear, except on the one point of the murder he felt he had committed. With one part of his memory, he recalled Tarleton Beamish's story and knew that he was not implicated in it; his own failing was to have abandoned Tart and run, to have made no effort to help him, to treat his wound, to get him back to safety. He had deserted. He had reached the end of his strength and run away, and though he knew the war was long over he was convinced that if he was found he would be tried and executed or imprisoned. Desertion under fire was not a forgivable offence.

He had these facts straight, and yet still, in dreams, in moments of exhaustion, when the strength he had spent months building up seemed suddenly to vanish, the vision would come back, of himself killing a girl and leaving her body in a dark corner of an ancient ruin. He could make no sense of the visitations, and they went on for years.

Edith watched her father's face as he talked about this nightmare he could not escape, and although she didn't speak the anger came back, that he was haunted by his guilt over the death of a dream child, but apparently untouched by his desertion of his own.

"But you, Edith, what about you?"

"I was growing up without a father."

A little rain fell against the windows of the room. In the darkness, the city told itself old stories, of power and the grandeur of empire, of treachery, of nobility and splendour, of poverty and degradation. She could feel the pressure of the low clouds, the beating of rain; the rain was full of ghosts. She was reminded of a primitive painting she had once seen of the plague in Trastevere, the neighbourhood just across the river, the streets full of dead bodies, the air above the city full of angels.

"Tell me. What it was like," he said again.

She began to talk, her throat dry and constricted. Her voice was harsh and ancient, and as she spoke she felt the past fall in pieces around her. Things happened, then other things, and afterward one gave those things names.

She stopped to ask a question. She had to know. Had he ever wanted to return to them? While she lived out the things she was telling, was her existence ever in his mind?

He tried to explain, struggling to get at a hard truth and not to adjust that truth too easily to what she wanted him to say. The easy explanation was that he wanted to return but feared being arrested as a deserter. But it was more complex than that. He kept the snapshot with him as a kind of talisman, a link to what he had loved some time in the past, but he had a new life as well. He had been baptized a Roman Catholic by Don Benedetto, and when the old man died he went to work for a monastery a few miles away as a labourer, carpenter, handyman.

Now neither one spoke. They had reached a kind of stillness. There was the sound of a car in the narrow street outside the apartment. Edith felt stupid with shock and exhaustion, wordless, almost without feeling. Her father rose from his chair, as if he might be about to make his way out into the night, but he came toward her, and Edith was caught in the gaze of his eyes. There was something fine about his face, that made her understand how a village boy, seeing him wounded, half dead, might take him for Christ.

He was beside her chair, and he was kneeling.

Edith stood and walked away.

"No," she said, "no kneeling, no touching gestures of forgiveness. Opera is for on stage, with an orchestra and scenery."

The old man was getting slowly to his feet. His eyes

were turned away. She had humiliated him. She went back to where he stood, looked in his eyes.

"There are some kinds of gesture I can't accept. I don't want to kneel or be knelt to. The only way I know to live is with my two feet planted firmly on the ground. And my eyes open. If you want, we will be friends, you and I, and if we're lucky, someday we'll find that the present is more important than the past. That's what I can offer. Do you think I'm hard and cold?"

She held out her hand to him, and he took it. Old as he was, and fragile looking, the hand that took hers was large and strong. She looked toward him, her eyes studying every detail of the heavy ridged scar that marked his face, and she tried to remember the face of that man who sat beside her on the bench in the park, explaining to a small girl why he had to go away to war.

"Do you remember," she said, "what you gave me when you went away?"

"A little silver heart."

Edith pulled out the chain she wore round her neck. The silver heart hung from it.

"You were more faithful than I was," he said.

"It doesn't just mean you, this little heart. It reminds me who I was and where I came from."

"Do you often go back?"

"Once recently. For Verna's funeral."

"Did she remarry?"

"No. Though she needed a husband. Do you remember Sid Appleton?"

"I remember the name."

"He came to dinner. They went to the movies together.

For years. He cried like a child at her funeral. But she never married him. Maybe somehow she knew you were still alive."

Ralph withdrew his hand and walked back to the sofa where he'd been sitting. He sat, rubbed his face with his left hand, hard, as if to pull the skin loose.

"I didn't want to go back to her," he said.

"You could have gone back and asked for a divorce."

"No. If I went back, I would have stayed."

"What was wrong between you?"

"Nothing that a hundred other people wouldn't have lived with happily enough. I just expected too much."

"So did I."

"You never married."

"There was no place for it in my life." She looked toward the corner where Ezio had fallen asleep in his chair. "And there was Ezio watching over me. And a man now and then if I wanted something warm in my bed."

It had grown light outside, the rain had ended, and from the street she heard the shouts of a gang of masons who were doing repairs on a building nearby, the façade of a seventeenth-century palazzo that was having apartments built into the remains of its rooms. She heard more noises from down the street where the merchants were starting to set up their market stalls in the piazza, under the brooding black statue of Giordano Bruno, who had been martyred here. Who had argued the existence of a multiplicity of worlds. The hood of his gown was drawn up over his head, his face bent forward in intense concentration. All around him, the square would be covered with piles of fruit, boxes of fish and shellfish, racks of fresh meat.

Edith went to the piano and picked up the snapshot which Ezio had put there after she let it fall to the floor. She looked at the face of the girl. She thought she could almost remember the day the photograph was taken. It was Vi who had taken it, and for some reason the idea of posing for a photograph to be sent to Ralph had made Verna terribly nervous. She kept making them wait while she went in the house to change her clothes one more time.

Edith studied the face of the little girl, but it told her nothing. She turned back to her father.

"I need to sleep," she said. "Do you want to come to my apartment?"

"Later. I have a room in a hotel. We'll sleep, and then we'll meet later."

They shook hands, rather formally, and Edith left. Instead of walking across to her own apartment, she took the few steps along the cobbled street to the square to buy some oranges at the market. Not all the stalls were open yet, but she found one with good oranges.

"*Buon giorno, signora*," the woman said to her with a wave. "*È venuta di buon' ora stamattina.*"

Edith nodded and asked for a kilo of the oranges. When she got home, she'd eat one or two and then fall asleep.

# Chapter 14

E major. French horns, bassoons, rampant, a dotted figure rising a sixth, then a fourth, settling for a moment down a tone, then rising another fourth to the tonic to declare the first three notes of the E major scale.

This is the opening night of the National Arts Centre Opera Festival, and in the audience there are members of the cabinet, deputy ministers, the leader of an opposition party, heads of two Crown corporations, and a school of lesser fish. The evening outside is balmy, but not hot, and many members of the audience have not come in until the last minute, choosing instead to walk by the canal in the evening sunlight. In the lobby, the tuxedos of the ministers (and the gay scarlet dress of the lady minister) are surrounded by assistants and disciples and a number of those who wish to be close without (they hope) appearing sycophantic. Everyone behaves with an assumed poise which masks a deep uneasiness. Entry to the seats, the darkening of the auditorium, the first notes from the orchestra, come as a blessed relief.

As the rich, slow, syncopated chords, the soaring, swooping, chromatic melody of the overture's coda pour over the audience, the curtain opens on the bedroom of the Marschallin. The colours are mostly muted greens and browns that seem constantly to approach the splendour of gold, but never to state it. Beyond the room's high windows, from which the morning light has begun to penetrate the darkness, is a formal garden, where a fruit tree is in blossom.

On the bed, just caught by the morning light, lie the Marschallin and her lover Octavian. The tall slender mezzo who sings Octavian is dressed in trousers and frilled shirt of a brilliant white. The Marschallin wears a gown of a rich plum colour which stands out as the only hint of red in the whole setting. The audience waits impatiently to hear the voice of this soprano, finally performing in her native country after a long career in Europe.

Her father had been silent, nervous, abrupt, through the whole trip. Twice he had insisted that the hired driver stop the car at service stations while he went to the toilet and bought gum or candy. He was like a recalcitrant child trying to delay their arrival. It was at his insistence that they were returning to the town he had fled many years before, but now that they were on their way he was uneasy to the point of petulance.

He was old. She remembered an energetic, thoughtful young man who had been misplaced somewhere, in the war or in the years after the war. Now he would be silent for long periods and then begin to fret over the gardens he'd left behind, whether they were being properly attended to in his absence, how inept most of the brothers were, lost without Ralph there to keep things in order. In the front seat, the man hired to drive them sat unspeaking. Her father had wanted to drive the car, but Edith refused because he had no licence. Her refusal made him sulky. Each time one of the fits of irritability struck him, she could see him catch himself, get the petulance under control, try to behave politely.

Along the sides of the road, the sun of the summer afternoon fell on fields of stubble where the hay had been taken off, on the dim gold of the ripe oats and wheat, on the deep late-summer green of trees and pasture. Cattle stood still in a field split by the curve of a slow, muddy creek. Ahead they could see the first houses of the town, a couple of church towers, new apartment blocks.

"It's like a dream," the old man beside her said. "You almost know it, but so many things don't fit."

"We've both been away a long time."

Baron Ochs has left the stage, with his characteristic heavy-handed courtesy, and the Marschallin contemplates the way of the world, how this old profligate is able to boast that he will honour a beautiful young girl by marrying her.

She must not let herself be troubled by this; it is only the way of the world.

The strings establish F major with a rather gay tune in 2/4. A small chamber orchestra, solo strings with clarinet, oboe and basoon, plays sixteen bars of this lively tune, and the Marshallin moves downstage, her movements slow and reflective as, thinking of Ochs's forthcoming marriage, she remembers her own. The lightness and gaiety of the accompaniment takes any taint of sentimentality from this remembrance of her younger self, her puzzlement that she is still the person who was once that innocent convent girl.

To perform the Marschallin, the singer has scaled down the size of her voice from what it might be for Tosca or Violetta, so that its sound will be poignant rather than passionate.

The music slows a little as the Marschallin realizes that there is also a future self hidden in her, an old woman, comic or pathetic, and the music slides down into E flat, but even here, in this new softer key, the gay little tune goes on, worldly and unthinking.

This soprano is older than Strauss's original idea – a married woman of thirty-two in love with a boy of seventeen – but there is a liveliness about her movements, a daintiness to her voice that allows her to carry the part.

Octavian enters, in riding-habit and boots, sensitive enough to feel immediately his lover's sadness, but too young and self-involved to understand it or offer comfort. He can only think that she is worried for him, and pursues this vision of himself beloved ("for me, for me") all the way to F sharp, then G sharp. He will weep at her sadness and force her to comfort him. He will be angry when she predicts, truly, that sooner or later Octavian must leave her.

"It was always lovely, getting your letters and knowing that you were doing such wonderful things. Travelling all over the world the way you do. Violet would have been so pleased."

The unseeing eyes were staring somewhere just a little to the left of Edith's face. Mabel was tiny now, and blind, but there was still a core of living energy.

"I could never have done it without the money Vi left me."

"She had such dreams, that girl. I was more of a stay-at-home, and I suppose I cramped her style. When she thought of it, sitting in that hospital bed one day, she turned round to me with such a smile on her face. You know that big smile of Violet's. She said did I mind if she didn't leave me her money, and I'll admit I was shocked for a minute. We'd always said we'd leave the money to each other, but I could see she had a bee in her bonnet, so I said she better tell me what it was all about. Well, she did, and that was the first time I'd seen her so happy from the day she got sick. It was wonderful to see. Of course I couldn't say no, could I?"

"You were very generous, Mabel."

"Edith, you've paid it back a hundred times. Knowing that you've done just what Violet would have wanted, and always writing me such letters. I'd take them down to Fullerton's when I was still working and read them aloud to the girls there. It's been a wonderful thing in my life. Violet always knew best, didn't she? Everybody said she was flighty and I was the sensible one, but she knew best."

There was a tiny flush of red on her pale, wrinkled cheeks, as if she might be a little feverish. The fine white hair had fallen forward and she felt it touch her face and brushed it impatiently away. There was a hairbrush on the dresser that stood under the large window, and Edith got up and fetched it.

"Here, Mabel," she said, "I'll brush back that hair."

Two or three strokes of the brush put the hair in place. As she was brushing it, Edith was aware how pale the scalp was, how thin the bones beneath it. As she put the brush away, Mabel's blind eyes tried to follow her movements. Edith sat back down in her chair. It was a comfortable chair. Everything in the room was clean and comfortable and bright. It was very unlike the dim cluttered house that Mabel and Violet had shared, a house where there seemed always a faint smell of old secrets, hidden motives, unspoken intensities. Did the old really want to be extracted from their settings, like teeth from ailing gums? Of course Mabel couldn't see what was around her, but she must sense it.

"I spoke to Verna about it, the money. You never knew how Verna would take things."

Edith couldn't find an answer. Her mother was still a subject forbidden her. She couldn't speak about her, could hardly think about her. To her father, she had said what had to be said and no more. At the heart of her life was an untouchable stranger. She had not loved her mother. Perhaps she had hated her. Certainly she had abandoned her, as quickly and as entirely as she could. When she took her father to the cemetery to show him the grave, she had hurried away and left him there. She had nothing to say. There was a coldness in Edith, somewhere, without which she would not have survived, and the thought of her mother roused that coldness.

"She wasn't a happy woman, that Verna. Even before she lost Ralph." Edith wondered if she should tell Mabel about her father, that he was here in town. No. "It was as if she had no gift for being happy. She'd look on the bad side of a sunny day sometimes."

It troubled Edith that she enjoyed hearing these words, that even now she wanted her mother lessened, criticized. Why couldn't she feel sympathy for her, poor pretty Verna Sinclair who'd married, so young, a man she would never understand, who'd been left alone with an eccentric, difficult daughter? Edith could say the words, but the coldness stayed. It was a part of her, and without it she would never have made the life she had.

Her mother was part of the past. Everything in this place was. Since she'd arrived in town, she'd half wanted to ask someone about David Lannan, but couldn't bring herself to it. Was he dead? His name had vanished from the phone book. For some reason, Edith was convinced that he had committed suicide.

"Is there anything you need, Mabel?" she said to the old woman opposite her. "Anything I can do for you?"

"There is one thing I'd like, Edith. I hope you don't mind. For me and for Violet too. I don't suppose she can see us here, but who's to say about things like that? But sitting here, listening to you talk, I was thinking how I'd like it if you could sing me a little something. Just to hear your voice. I'll never get to one of those famous places where they come to hear you sing, will I? Maybe you could do what you sang at the school that time. Violet and I often talked about that."

"Of course I'll sing for you, Mabel."

She found the pitch and began.

The large reception room is pale blue, and beyond its

windows is a sky of the deep perfect blue of summer morning. In the middle of the room, Sophie waits for the beautiful stranger to present her with the silver rose sent as a token of betrothal by the still unseen, still therefore magical figure of her soon-to-be husband, Baron Ochs. She is about to fall irretrievably in love with the rose-bearer, the messenger.

Octavian, who brings the rose, is all in silver, and as he enters a wavering series of chromatic chords on flute, celeste and harp at the top of their range drops slowly and gently down, like a glittering silver rain. This shimmer of sound will return all through the scene as the two lovers find each other's eyes and are lost in delight. With Octavian's first words, the oboe declares its lyrical love theme in dotted triplets.

That Octavian is acted and sung by a beautiful woman only increases the sense of benign impersonality, inevitability. This is Love. It is not conditioned by familiarity or good sense, or even gender. It is the appetite of the young for involvement in the beauty and passion of life. It is the presentation of a silver rose. It is the sparkling exultation of the highest range of flute, celeste and harp.

Her destination was a long cab ride from downtown Toronto, and Edith wondered, as the cab made its way through unfamiliar streets, whether the outing wasn't altogether quixotic, but Nancy Longridge had written her twice after she had heard the news that Edith was coming back to Canada and urged her to visit. Now the possibility of future engagements had brought Edith to the city, and it had seemed natural enough to dial the number she had been given. She was curious. Nancy and her husband had fled Rome very abruptly, and once they were gone it became clear to Edith how much she had counted on her lessons with Nancy to shape the empty time. And the voice itself was so marvellous. She cared to know what had become of the girl.

The cab driver pulled up in front of a brick bungalow, one of a group of similar houses on a curving street. It wasn't a new area, yet Edith was sure it had been built, this whole neighbourhood had been built, after she'd left Toronto for Europe. Might Carl now live in a neighbourhood like this? No. By now he would have done better than this very ordinary suburb.

Edith looked along the street as the cab drove away. Children playing on a paved driveway. A woman in a plastic lawn chair on a concrete porch, surveying the flat lawn in front of her. A few, mostly sickly, trees. Climbing roses. Pansies and petunias. Some of the lawns a little yellow. One still very green, a sprinkler running. Men and women lived on this street that she had never before seen or imagined. Lives were spent here. The world went on being the world, whether she willed it or not.

She went up the path and climbed three steps to the door of the house. In her purse was a present for the baby Nancy was carrying. A music box: it seemed appropriate.

She rang the bell, the door was opened to her, and she was inside the house, observing, assessing. The furniture was oddly assorted, an old stuffed couch with a modern wood and glass coffee table in front of it, an ugly low piano stacked with music, an old rocking-chair, a second-hand bookshelf filled with texts and paperbacks, television on its altar in the corner. Over the couch, a large and colourful theatre poster stuck in place with pieces of masking tape. It was confused and temporary, the reflection of no particular taste.

Nancy stood in front of her, belly swollen, her face a little rounded by pregnancy, a smile that seemed real and comfortable. This odd girl, commonplace, riddled by flashes of brilliance, had made a nest here. Edith was struck by the bravery of it all, this street of little houses in which hundreds of people lived out lives in which, behind a surface of convention, all manner of complicated daily struggles passed by. These remarkable bungalows would outlast the people in them, who would carry their struggle to the doors of extinction and pass through, to be replaced by their children and grandchildren. It was nothing, and it was everything.

Nancy was hugging her. Hugging her and crying, and Edith could feel the hard lump that was the baby pressing against her own body.

"Stop this blubbering," Edith said. "I didn't come here to be cried on."

"I thought you'd be too mad to come."

"Why?"

"I thought you'd be so disappointed in me."

"What a silly girl you are."

"Studying with you, those weeks in Rome, was…such a wonderful thing. The most wonderful thing ever. But…that wasn't me, not really."

"Is this you, the real person, pregnant and weeping?"

The girl laughed.

"I never used to cry," she said. "Maybe it's just one of the symptoms. I keep discovering new ones. And you were right. I'm singing better than ever."

"Where do you sing?"

"In a church here. Quite a big one. Solos with a couple of other groups. Lots to keep me busy."

"And Lee?" Edith asked, not wanting to know. Hateful man, destroyer.

"He's working in one of the Church missionary offices. Probably in a few years he'll study to be ordained. Everything's fine now."

Fine for him, Edith reflected. She took a seat on the couch and Nancy lowered herself into an old rocking-chair opposite her, a cushion behind her back.

"I wish I could get to Ottawa to hear you sing," Nancy said.

"I may sing in Toronto next year."

"Good. I'm glad you came back out of retirement."

Oddly phrased, but how else to put it?

"I decided I have a few more years."

The girl was beaming at her.

"I can't quite believe I've got you here. In my own house. That I can make you coffee and cookies and talk to you like friends."

Edith remembered how very much she liked this girl.

"It's strange to be back in Toronto," she said.

"It must have changed a lot."

"More than I could have imagined. What I like best is the parts that haven't changed. I want it to be the city I left thirty years ago."

"I think about that, you know. How you left and went away on your own. You must have been so brave."

"Or desperate."

"I can't imagine you being desperate. You're so...on top of things."

"Am I?"

"Compared with me. But I don't mind. Of course I never now what I'm going to feel next. You know what it's like when you're pregnant. Or I guess you don't," she said, laughing again, rocking her chair backward. She looked bright and shiny and innocent and full of love.

"I do know," Edith said, able to, now. "I do know what it's like to be pregnant."

Nancy laughed harder, as if Edith had told a joke, and then the laughter died, and the chair stopped rocking. She looked puzzled and disturbed, and Edith wanted to hug her and tell her not to worry.

"Did you...?"

It was strange to Edith how comfortable she felt in this small, half-decorated living room.

Her son probably lived somewhere in this city. He could be on this street. She might see him and never know it.

She wanted Nancy Longridge to know about her son.

"I had a baby once," Edith said. She could tell the story. How astonishing.

The Marschallin stands at the door of the room, ready to leave. The room in the inn is a little dim, the walls and floors of dark wood, and the Marschallin's gown, in shades of soft pearly grey with a touch of white trim at the bodice, glows coolly against the darkness. In the centre of the stage stands Octavian, his saffron coat vivid against the white of his breeches and the pale but intense green of Sophie's dress.

The final great trio of the opera begins with the Marschallin introducing the key of D flat major and the return of 3/4 time as she sings of how she has vowed to love Octavian rightly, even to love his love for another woman; still, it is almost too soon, almost too hard. Then the voice of Sophie enters, changing the key as she sings about her feeling that she might be in church, her innocent girl's sense that there is something holy in such deep emotion. Then quickly the voice of Octavian enters, asking questions, wanting someone to tell him what to do, torn between the two women, wanting to be loyal to the Marschallin, but struck down by his love for Sophie. Egocentric, blundering, just like a man.

The voices of the three twine together, the interlocking of three monologues, settled now in D flat, until, at the moment of the trio's climax, each of the voices at the top of its range, the key shifts, abruptly, to E major — for Strauss, the key of sincere love — then after four bars settles back into flats, the trio ends, and the Marschallin intones her last phrase, "in God's name," to a familiar sighing tune that has been heard since the orchestral introduction, and, giving one last look at her beloved Octavian, she leaves the stage.

The lovers sing on, and then, at the end of their duet, they too move off the stage, together. But Sophie has dropped her handkerchief, and it lies in the middle of the large dark room, a tiny white embroidered cloth that carries with it hints of a whole history of storytelling, of lost handkerchiefs and lovers' intrigues. It lies there, a last suggestion that no story is ever over.

Then a door opens. In come a little black page with a lighted taper in his hand. He looks for the handkerchief, finds it, trips out.

The curtain falls.